**新文京開發出版股份有限公司**

NEW WCDP 新世紀‧新視野‧新文京 ─ 精選教科書‧考試用書‧專業參考書

New Wun Ching Developmental Publishing Co., Ltd.

New Age · New Choice · The Best Selected Educational Publications — NEW WCDP

職場英文

English for Specific Workplace

第二版
2nd edition

陳愛華 編著

編者的話

　　和業界產學合作已經邁入第五個年頭，編者深深感覺台灣傳產業經營的艱辛，以及業者亟需走向國際的渴望。在此過程，也瞭解傳產業因為產品品質優良且信用卓著，在國際上有相當的競爭力，然而大多數從業人員在職場相關的英語能力普遍有待提升。有些初進入職場的年輕人，也因對於英語能力的恐慌，在職場中未能取得應有的職涯發展成果，殊為可惜。

　　二版新增「發音練習」、「工業衛生與安全」、「廢棄物處理」、「員工在職訓練」及「產品設計與製造」等內容，並於書末加入課後練習，內容更加豐富。

　　結合與業者長期深入合作的實際經驗，特別以「情境式會話」方式，整理出傳產業與國際客戶的往來互動以及內部經營管理的 20 項單元，使用淺顯實用的英文說明各真實情境，提供實務應對（用）表達內容；也針對產品功能示範及職場相關業務操作流程，以實際的案例說明；另整理各單元中重要及常用的單字字彙與片語，便於使用者加強練習；較為特殊的是，編者提出特別的單字音節發音法，讓學習者能快速且正確的唸出單字的發音，與客戶或同儕有良好的溝通。希望年輕的學子以及傳產業的從業人員，經由研習本書能熟習傳產業相關的專業英文內容，得以強化在職場的競爭力，更能促進傳產業在國際上的蓬勃發展。

編者簡介

　　作者陳愛華老師畢業於美國賓州印第安那大學，擁有英語教學博士學位。她在修平科技大學及其前身樹德工商專科學校擔任英文教師已超過二十餘載，並且在國內外期刊發表多篇與英語教學有關的研究論文。陳老師對英語教學充滿熱忱，將多年英語教學經驗與業界實務應用結合，期盼能盡一己之力，略協助學子提升英文能力，增加國人在國際發展的競爭力，是為所願。

誌 謝

　　特別感謝「諭成有限公司」陳招銘董事長提供長期的產學合作機會，並指導業者的實務發展需求方向，以及公司相關同仁積極參與且提出實際的職場情境狀況，增加本書內容的豐富度。也感謝修平科技大學應用英語系校友邱婉菁博士及李宜芳小姐、修平科技大學上銀科技專班的同學、以及臺灣真空鍍膜股份有限公司執行董事陳彥伯先生等人，協助提供寶貴的參考資料，增益本書的實用性。在此，一併謹致上最大的感謝。

本書特色

- 真實的傳產現場呈現。
- 著重討論式的學習方法。
- 詳細的英文單字解釋。
- 獨特的單字音節發音學習法。劃底線的音節代表重音，沒有音節的單字表示該單字為單音節。
- 補充說明部分，加強對職場特定業務的認識。

如何使用本書

- 強化英文能力的基本要求是英文單字量要夠。學生盡量熟記本書整理的「字彙及片語」，授課教師可以於每周上課時，花 10 分鐘考英文單字，以督促學生勤背單字。
- 單字除了會拼寫及發音外，最重要的是知道如何使用該單字，教師可以協助學生用單字或片語學習造句。
- 熟悉會話內容後，學生做角色扮演活動或課堂討論，增加師生互動機會。
- 教師指導學生分組蒐集傳統產業現況，將實際的職場情況融入於課堂學習。

目錄
Contents

PART 3 產品功能示範及職場相關業務操作流程   **156**

英文熱身操
—發音練習

PART

1

　　音標包含母音及子音。母音有長、短之分，而子音又分成有聲子音及無聲子音兩種。有聲和無聲子音的區別是：有聲子音發音時聲帶會振動，而無聲子音發音時聲帶不會振動。

一、母音

/e/: bake, cake, fate, gate, hate, lake, make, tape

bait, paint, rain, wait

day, may, pay, ray, say

paper

/ɛ/: bed, bet, get, jet, let, net, pet, set, vet, wet, yet

said

/æ/: ant, bad, bat, cat, fat, gap, lag, mad, mat, pat, sad, sat, tap

---

/i/: eel, green, heel, leek, meet, seek, sheep, sheet

beach, eat, heal, hear, heat, read, seat

/I/: bitch, ear, it, hill, hit, kick, mitt, rid, ship, shit, sick, sit

/a/: cock, dot, hot, not, pot, spot, top, topic

car, part, star, start, tart

/ʌ/: one, come, dove, glove, love, some

but, cut, duck, fuzz, gut, hut, lust, must, nut, rust, son, sun

/ə/: admire, ago, Amanda, apartment, drama, panda

/ɜ/: bird, burn, dirty, girl, hurt, Kurt, word, work, worm

/ɚ/: brother, doctor, teacher

/u/: boot, food, goose, mood, noodle, rood, tooth

/ʊ/: cook, foot, good, goods, hood, wood

/o/: code, coke, joke, lope, mode, note, nose, pole, poke

quote, robe, rode, rope, rose, sole, spoke, tote, vote

cold, old

know, snow

/ɔ/: cock, dog, hot, pot, top, spot, topic, storm, walk, warm

雙母音

/aɪ/: bike, bite, hike, kite, like, lime, mike, pile, rime, site

vice, vine, while, wife, wine, write

die, lie, pie

light, might, night, right, fight

bye, dye, eye

grind, minor, wind

buy, by, I, my

/aʊ/: cow, now, our, owl, wow

/ɔɪ/: boy, oil, soil, toy

二、子音

無聲子音

/p/: pan, pat, pay, pea, pun, lap, mop, rip, rope, tap

/t/: tie, to, two, beat, hit, late, root

/k/: class, come, could, Kate, back, luck, peck, pick

有聲子音

/b/: ban, bat, bay, bee, bun, lab, mob, rib, robe, tab

/d/: dare, dear, deer, die, do, hid, laid, ride, rude

/g/: gate, glass, good, gum, bag, lug, peg, pig

無聲子音

/f/: face, fast, ferry, fine, leaf, knife, roof, safe

/θ/: thank, thick,thief, thin, think, three, through, math

/s/: sack, see, sink, sit, snack, snake, peace, ox

/ʃ/: sheet, shit, shoes, shop, should, shoulder, fish, wash

sugar, ocean

/h/: home, horse, hose, hot, house, how

有聲子音

/v/: have, leave, move, save, vase, vast, very, vine

/ð/: brother, father, feather, leather, than, that, the, this

/z/: zeal, zebra, zip, zipper, Jazz, lazy, quiz, zigzag

/ʒ/: decision, leisure, occasion, pleasure, usual

無聲子音

/ʧ/: chest, chip, much, question

architecture, funiture, future, manufacture

有聲子音

/ʤ/: age, cage, change, Jack, judge, jump, just, loung

有聲子音

/m/: mat, meet, monk, month, mood, moth,mouse, mouth

/n/: nap, neck, need, nod, nose, Nick, knee, knock

/ŋ/: along, drink, long, lung, ring, sing, song

/w/: want, ward, way, wide, wig, wood

/j/: yacht, yarn, yawn, yell, yellow, yes

情境式會話
Situational conversation

PART

2

UNIT 01 Client Reception 客戶接待

Useful expressions

1. Do you have an appointment with Mr. Chen?

2. Do you need a ride to our office?

3. You can park your car in space number 2 of zone B in the basement.

4. Here are the samples of our products.

5. Are you interested in visiting other companies who cooperate with us?

6. It's on the fifth floor. You can take the elevator next to the water fountain in the corner.

7. The restroom is down the hallway and on the left hand side.

8. Thank you for your visit. Have a good day.

Words and phrases

appointment （尤指正式的）約會	ride 搭乘	zone 地區
be interested in 對...感興趣	cooperate 合作	elevator 電梯
next to 在...旁邊	water fountain 飲水機	hallway 走廊

Dialogue

Monday morning, Lily is just informed that a foreign client is coming to visit their company. She has a lot of work to take care of that day so she asks a colleague, Jill, to help her receive this guest.

Lily: Well, I've just learned that a foreign client is coming to visit us around ten this morning. I have accumulated a lot of work over the past two weeks and have to take care of it in time. Could you please help me receive this visitor when he's here? I'll be right with you after I've finished my work.

Jill: I'd like to help you but I'm afraid that my English is not good enough for a reception.

Lily: Don't worry. You will have no problem. Just remember: smiling courteously is a successful means of communication. I think the good strategy for receiving guests is to give them warm hospitality and make them feel at home. Anyway, I'll be with you as soon as possible.

Jill: All right. I'll try my best.

At about ten, the intercom signals.

Jill: Hello, How may I help you?

Matt: Hi, this is Matt from ABC Company. Could you please open the door?

Jill: Oh, yes. One moment please.

> *Jill is walking to the gate to receive Matt; at the same time, the door is unlocked and opens automatically.*

Jill: Hello, Mr. Lurk. Welcome to EZ Company. I'm Jill. Nice to meet you.

Matt: Nice to meet you too, Jill. Please call me Matt.

Jill: The reception room is on the second floor. This way please.

> *They go up to the reception room.*

Jill: Here it is. Please have a seat. The administrators are all in a meeting now which will be over in a minute.

Matt: I'm sorry. I'm a little bit early. The traffic was good this morning.

Jill: You're lucky. Would you like a cup of tea or coffee?

Matt: Tea is fine, thanks.

Jill: What kind of tea would you like? Oolung, Pu'er, green, black, or herbal tea?

Matt: Oolung please.

Jill: Ok, I'll be back in just a moment.

A few minutes later, Jill comes back carrying a tray with tea.

Jill: Here's your Oolung tea. It's hot. I'll put it on the table.

Matt: Thank you very much.

Jill: Have you been to Taiwan before?

Matt: Actually, it's my first time. I'm a representative in the Asian area. I usually visit Thailand and China.

Jill: How long are you staying here?

Matt: I'm going to be here for one week. For the first three days, I'm going to visit three companies. After that, I'd like to travel around the island.

When they are chatting, Lily and the boss come to meet Matt.

Richard: Hello, Mr. Lurk. My name is Richard; I'm the general manager of this company. Welcome to our company. Here's my business card.

Matt: Thank you, Richard. Here's mine. Nice to see you.

Richard: Nice to see you too. This is Lily. Do you know her?

Lily: Hi, Matt. I'm Lily. Nice to see you. We've e-mailed several times and at last we meet each other.

Matt: Yes. It seems we've known each other for a while.

Richard: So, how was your trip to Taiwan?

Matt: It's a long flight but the trip was fine. Taiwanese people are very friendly and helpful.

Richard: Thank you for your compliments. I would like to know if you are free this evening. If so, we'd like to treat you for dinner.

Matt: You are so kind. I'm free after four o'clock today.

Richard: That's great. Lily, could you make a reservation at the restaurant for dinner? Ask them to reserve a table for ten of us and we'll be there at six. Mr. Lurk, I'll pick you up at your hotel around 5:30 pm. Will that be ok?

Matt: That's fine. I'll be ready by then. Thanks again for your hospitality.

Powerful word bank

inform 告知	client 客戶	colleague 同事
receive 接待	accumulate 累積	reception 接待
courteously 有禮貌地	means 方法	strategy 策略
hospitality 款待	intercom 對講機	signal 發信號
unlock 開啟	automatically 自動地	administrator 行政官員
herbal 草本的	representative 代表	compliment 恭維
treat 款待	reserve 保留	

Useful phrases

in time 及時	at the same time 同時	reception room 會客室
general manager 總經理	business card 名片	make a reservation 預約
pick up 用汽車接某人	by then 到那時	

Discussion

1. What etiquette does the receptionist require having?

2. What subjects can the receptionist talk about with the visitors?

3. If you were a visitor, what kind of reception would you like to have?

4. What position does English have in the workplace?

5. What are the conventional industries in Taiwan?

Supplementary information

Tips for receiving clients on business

· Maintain a friendly smile.

· Exchange business cards.

· Shake hands firmly.

· Have eye contact.

- Serve tea or coffee.

- Make appropriate conversation.

- Escort the guests to the intended place.

- Offer a ride to places.

- Plan a short trip to a scenic spot.

- Give a localized and unique gift.

MEMO

UNIT 02 Presentation Skills
簡報技巧

Useful expressions

1. Good morning, ladies and gentlemen. Welcome to our company.

2. I'm going to give a 15-minute presentation.

3. There are three parts to the presentation.

4. They include: when our company started,

5. what products we produce,

6. and how we cooperate with our business partners.

7. If you have any questions, please feel free to ask.

8. That's all for the presentation.

9. Thanks for listening.

10. Do you have any questions?

Words and phrases

presentation 介紹	include 包括	product 產品
produce 生產		

Dialogue

A foreign client, Mr. Smith, is going to visit EZ Company in two weeks. A group of people is talking about this event.

Richard: Kelly, when is Mr. Smith coming to visit us?

Kelly: He said in his previous e-mail that he would be here on Thursday, July 20th.

Richard: Do you know what time he will arrive? I think we need to prepare for his visit properly.

Kelly: Yes. It's his first time visiting us. I'd like to make a presentation for him first. I'm currently working on the presentation.

Richard: Great. Let me know if you need any help.

Later on, when Kelly is busy preparing her presentation, her supervisor, Lily, passes by and Kelly asks her for help.

Kelly: Hi, Lily. Mr. Smith is coming to visit us and I'm going to give him a presentation about our company. I don't have much experience at making presentations. Could you give me some advice?

Lily: Well, you'll be fine. We've all gone through that stage. When you are making the presentation, not only does the content need to be thorough, you also have to present it fluidly. In addition, before starting the presentation, you have to greet the audience with a friendly smile and good eye contact. Then, introduce yourself first including your name and which departments you work in.

Kelly: Do I need to dress up that day?

Lily: Wearing the uniform is okay. By the way, after greeting the guest, you need to tell him what you are going to say and that the presentation will be limited to 15 minutes.

Kelly: Yes, I will briefly introduce the organization of the company and the products we produce. I will emphasize the best features of our products in order to impress the audience.

Lily: So, what will you do after the presentation?

Kelly: If the visitor still has time, I'll give him a factory tour. Is that okay?

Lily: Yes, that's a very good idea. Good luck on your first shot.

Powerful word bank

event 事件	previous 先前的	properly 恰當地
supervisor 監督人	content 內容	thorough 周密的
present 提出	fluidly 流暢地	greet 問候
audience 觀眾	briefly 簡潔地	organization 組織
emphasize 強調	feature 特色	impress 使感動

Useful phrases

make a presentation 做簡報

pass by 經過

in addition 此外

eye contact 眼神接觸

dress up 穿上盛裝

factory tour 工廠參觀

first shot 首次嘗試

Discussion

1. How do you skillfully make a presentation?

2. What is the purpose of making a presentation?

3. What topics can a presentation be made in?

4. If a presenter doesn't prepare the presentation well, as a listener, how do you feel about it?

5. If a presenter can only present the slides but cannot answer questions about his/her presentation, as a listener, how do you feel about it?

Supplementary information

Tips for making a presentation

· Each PowerPoint slide should not have too many words.

· The background color of the slides needs to be soft and clear.

· Give the audience the outline of the presentation at the beginning.

- Don't read off the slides line by line.

- Face the audience with smile.

- Use a pointer instead of the index finger to the targeted point.

- Limit the presentation to between 12 and 15 minutes.

Organization of a company

Finance & Accounting Department (Dept.)財務部

Sales Dept.業務部(may include selling, marketing, and logistics)

Packaging Dept.包裝部

Production Dept.生管部

Plant Affairs Dept.廠務部

QC(quality control) Dept.品管部

Research and Development (R&D) Dept.開發部

Warehouse Dept.倉管部

Materials Dept.資材部

Factory tour English　工廠導覽英語

1. Please watch your step.

2. The factory is very noisy. Do you need the earplugs?

3. This is the production line.

4. Our company was founded in 2008. There are about 80 employees now.
   我們在 2008 年設廠，目前大約有 80 名員工。

5. Here is the R&D Department.
   這裡是開發部門。

6. We are the OEM (original equipment manufacturer) for many companies. Our major market is the U.S. followed by Europe and Asia.
   我們幫很多客戶代工。我們的產品主要是外銷美國，其次是歐洲及亞洲。

UNIT 03 Factory Inspection 驗廠

Useful expressions

1. Here's the document you requested.

2. Which department would you like to inspect first?

3. Watch your step when you are in the factory.

4. Do you need a gauge?

5. When will I receive the evaluation?

6. The inspectors certified by SGS usually inspect our factory several times a year.

7. An inspector designated by one of our clients is coming to inspect our factory.

8. I need to do a lot of paperwork for the inspection.

Words and phrases

document 文件	request 要求	inspect 檢查
watch your step 留心您的腳步	gauge 測量儀器	evaluation 評估
certify 證實	designate 委任	

Dialogue

Two official inspectors are authorized by one of EZ company's clients to examine the area of the factory. They are from Germany and have been to the company many times already.

Lily: Hi, Christopher. Nice to see you again.

Chris: Hi, Lily. Nice to see you. This is Ben and it's his first time in Taiwan.

Lily: Nice to meet you, Ben. Welcome to Taiwan and EZ company.

Ben: Thank you and nice to meet you, too.

Chris: Well, Lily, could you give us a tour of the factory now?

Lily: Sure. This way, please. I'll show you the production area first, then, the Research and Development Department.

Chris: Thank you very much.

After the tour, Lily brings them to the show room and two inspectors walk around there to take a look at the displayed objects.

Chris: There are many different hand tools here. So, your company mainly cooperates with the OEM. Where are those companies you are working with located?

Lily: Most of our products are exported to Asian and European countries. And some to the U.S. The logos on the wall are those of the companies we've cooperated with.

Chris: Apparently, your boss works very hard to expand the business. I remember that there was only one factory when I came here for the first time two years ago. And there are two factories now. And the number of factory workers is growing as well.

Lily: Yes, our boss is a very ambitious person who tries to give his employees a bright future, so he's been really working very hard these past few years.

Chris: When we were in the production area, I found that ventilation there is poor.

Lily: Oh, well, I'll inform the relevant office to improve it immediately. Thank you very much for your input.

Chris: Thanks for your time. Now, can we go back to the conference room? I need to write a report about this inspection. And I will give you the evaluation later.

Lily: Sure, this way, please. Do you need a computer to work on your report? Or any stationery?

Chris: Thank you. I have my own laptop with me. I need to print something out later. So, maybe you can help me with that.

Lily: No problem. Here we are. I won't disturb you. Just ring me when you finish your work.

Chris: Sure.

Powerful word bank

official 正式的	authorize 授權給	examine 檢查
Germany 德國	display 陳列	object 物體
mainly 主要地	locate 把...設置在	export 輸出
logo 標識	apparently 顯然地	expand 擴充
ambitious 有雄心的	ventilation 通風	relevant 有關的
immediately 直接地	input 投入	stationery 文具
laptop 筆記型電腦	disturb 打擾	ring 打電話

Useful phrases

show room 展覽室	take a look at 看一看
OEM(Original Equipment Manufacturer) 委託代工	
conference room 會議室	

Discussion

1. How do people accomplish the entire factory inspection affair?

2. Why does the factory need to be inspected regularly?

Supplementary information

Entire factory inspection operation

Preprocess 前置作業

- Make sure the defects presented in the previous inspection have been improved.

- Prepare the obligatory subjects, paperwork, (and) data which the inspectors may request to check well.

- Plan and rehearse the flow of inspection, such as making the presentation, (doing the) factory tour, and so on.

- Give the inspectors a good impression of the good preparation, such as the cheerful office atmosphere, graceful manners, friendly greetings, a clean and orderly environment.

In progress 進行中

- Pay attention to the inspectors' talk.

- Take notes while escorting the inspectors touring the factory.

- Instantly provide the requested document.

Post-process 後續報告

- Learn the results of the evaluation.

- Give constructive opinions about the defects.

- Improve exactly the less than ideal aspects, such as ventilation and staff quarters.

- File and label all paperwork carefully.

- Maintain the records and keep them well organized.

SGS

　　是一個總部設在瑞士日內瓦的跨國集團，專門提供檢驗、鑑定、測試及認證服務。

Reply to the audit report 1　回覆驗廠報告範例之一

1. Disqualified items were not recorded specifically in the inspection form.
   不合格的產品，沒有在檢驗表格做詳細記錄。
   Those disqualified items have been specifically recorded in the form.
   已在檢驗表格詳細記錄。
   Afterword, each disqualified item will be recorded specifically in the designated form.
   之後如有不合格的產品時，將會詳細記錄在檢驗表格。

2. The containers for semi-finished products were not marked clearly.
   半成品的容器沒有明顯標示清楚。
   The containers for semi-finished products have been marked clearly.
   已在半成品的容器標示清楚。
   The containers for semi-finished products will be marked clearly afterword.
   之後會把半成品的容器標示清楚。

3. Defective products were not noted down in the designated form.

    不良品沒有寫不良品處理單。

    Defective products have been noted down in the designated form.

    已有寫不良品處理單。

    All defective products will be noted down in the designated form afterword.

    之後有不良品時，會寫不良品處理單。

4. Hazardous substances were not marked and examined by inspectors.

    沒有標示危險物質及沒有請檢驗人員做檢測。

    Hazardous substances have been marked and examined by inspectors.

    已在危險物質標示，並請檢驗人員做檢測。

    Hazardous substances will be marked and examined regularly afterword.

    之後都會標示危險物質，並定期做檢測。

Reply to the audit report 2　回覆驗廠報告範例之二

On January 27, 2016, we requested an architect to inspect the on-site area of the factory. Under the normal usage without changing the building construction, the building conforms to public safety regulations. Because of the land category, we are not able to report the inspection of building's public safety. However, the concerned authority has been making temporary factory registration open to public access year by year. At present, it is opened to those founded by March 2008 to apply. Our factory was built in 2011, thus, we are not allowed to apply for the inspection of building's public safety yet.

　　我司 105 年 1 月 27 日有請建築師勘查現場，公司在正常使用並不更動建築物構造體情形下，我司建築物公共安全檢測是安全的，但因地目的關係，所以無法申報建築物公共安全檢測。日後政府會逐年開放申請臨時廠登，現今已開放到 97 年 3 月可申請臨時廠登，但因我司是 100 年蓋好的，因此目前無法申報建築物公共安全檢測。

UNIT 04 Industrial Health and Safety 工業衛生與安全

Useful expressions

1. There's a lot of black smoke in the air and many fire trucks are going to the scene of the fire.

2. Flames shot out from a factory made of metal sheet a few minutes ago.

3. All employees are required to take first aid training, just in case they need self-help or need to help others.

4. Severe fire causes loss of life and property.

5. Smoking is prohibited indoors. Smokers cannot smoke unless they are in the designated area.

6. If the ground is slippery, a warning sign should be placed near it.

7. The office and factory have been equipped with a sprinkler system and smoke detectors.

Words and phrases

fire truck 救火車	scene of the fire 火場	flame 火焰
shoot out 像子彈一般衝出	metal sheet 鐵皮	in case 以防萬一
self-help 自助	cause 引起	loss property 財產損失
prohibit 禁止	indoors 在室內	unless 除非
designated area 指定的範圍	ground 地面	slippery 滑的
warning sign 警告標誌	place 放置	be equipped with 配備有…
sprinkler system 自動噴水滅火系統	smoke detector 煙霧探測器	

Dialogue

Lately, many industrial accidents have happened around the island and caused serious damage to property and human lives. In order to prevent the factory from suffering from disaster, special assistant, Christine, convenes a meeting to discuss these events.

Christine: As you know, there are many frequent industry accidents currently happening. I need to ask you for your help. I would like to set up five categories to work on: fire safety, environmental monitoring, employees' health, product labeling, and a building's public safety. Could you please give your valuable opinions?

David: I'm in charge of factory affairs and I regularly check the required signs and systems of fire safety, such as emergency exit lights, escape guide lights, fire detectors, fire alarms, and evacuation plans on the wall. The building materials are fireproof or have fireproof coating. I also update the fire equipment and fire extinguishers so that they're valid. I think it's very efficient to make a checklist for individually examined items. Nevertheless, smoking is prohibited in the factory. There are signs posted on the wall to remind workers not to smoke. And everybody is very cooperative.

Christine: Good job. Preventive measures do reduce the occurrence of serious accidents. By the way, environmental monitoring and cleanliness are very important, too. We have requested the relevant inspection authorities to carry out toluene environmental monitoring regularly. And, in the interest of sanitation, the factory has a perfect system of recycling.

James: The company also cares very much about employees' health and intends to maintain a clean working environment. An oily and slippery ground is not allowed in the factory. And the walkways and loading and unloading areas should be kept clear at all times. Also, there are first aid kits in several locations in case people need them. The automated external defibrillators are also set up in public places with an obvious hanging red sign "AED" above the device.

Christine: Well, it seems that we are well equipped for safety. Last time we were told that we ignored the required physical examination for the workers who engaged in noisy areas and flammable liquids areas. How's it going now?

Penny: That drawback has been corrected. Those workers will have their required health examination annually.

Christine: Great. By the way, how do workers work with the machines? Are they familiar with the operation processes?

David: People who work with the machines will take the training program first. And they will be supervised by a senior worker while they are using the machine. When have gotten used to using a machine, they can work independently. We also provide a prepared detailed operation manual next to the machine. So it is quite handy for the operator.

Christine: Ok, now, the next thing to discuss is the defective items labeling. Please inform the colleagues in your department that they have to make sure to note down any disqualified items on a designated form. The containers for semi-finished products should be marked clearly. In particular, hazardous substances need be marked and examined regularly.

David, James, and Penny nod their heads and say, "Yes, we'll pass this message on to our colleagues."

Christine: Well, now, the last thing is the issue of the building's public safety. Our company did not apply for the building's public safety inspection when it was established. We have authorized an architect to make all required applications and the building will be inspected regularly. In addition, for safety reasons, the staff quarters set up in the factory will be abandoned. The company will rent apartments nearby for the migrant workers.

Penny: The security measures are on track now so we can feel safe and focus on our work.

David: We still need to regularly take the required examination to ensure industrial safety.

Powerful word bank

industrial 工業的	accident 事故	damage 損害
prevent 防止	disaster 災害	convene 召集
frequent 時常發生的	category 種類	regularly 定期地
fireproof 防火的	coating 塗層	update 更新
valid 有效的	checklist 核對清單	nevertheless 然而

PART **②**

preventive 預防的	measures 措施	occurrence 發生
cleanliness 潔淨	authority 管理機構	toluene 甲苯
sanitation 公共衛生	oily 油的	walkway 走道
location 位置	obvious 明顯的	hanging 掛著的
device 裝置	ignore 忽視	noisy 嘈雜的
flammable 易燃的	liquid 液體	drawback 缺點
independently 獨立地	manual 手冊	handy 便利的
operator 操作者	defective 有缺陷的	disqualified 使不合格
container 容器	hazardous 有危險的	substance 物質
nod 點頭	establish 建立	architect 建築師
abandon 丟棄	rent 租用	ensure 保證

Useful phrases

set up 建立	work on 從事
environmental monitoring 環境監測	product labeling 產品標誌
such as 例如	emergency exit light 緊急出口燈
escape guide light 逃生引導燈	fire detector 火警探測器
fire alarm 火警警報器	evacuation plan 逃生配置圖
fire extinguisher 滅火器	carry out 執行

in the interest of 為了…	loading and unloading area 裝／卸貨區
keep clear 保持通暢	at all times 隨時
automated external defibrillator 自動體外心臟去顫器	operation process 操作步驟
senior worker 資深員工	next to 在…旁邊
make sure 確定	note down 記下
semi-finished product 半成品	in particular 尤其是
in addition 此外	on track 正軌；進入狀況
focus on 集中於	

Discussion

1. How can you prevent a fire from happening?

2. Why do people wear hard hats when they go to a construction site?

 **MEMO**

UNIT 05 Waste Treatment 廢棄物處理

Useful expressions

1. How do you take care of waste in your company?

2. A cooperative licensed waste treatment company will come to our company regularly to remove the waste.

3. In the process of manufacturing hand tools, a lot of scrap iron and iron filings will come out.

4. The price for the scrap iron recycling is much cheaper than the raw material.

5. After treatment, a lot of waste can be reused effectively. It's one way of reducing the amount of waste and protecting the environment.

6. The government regulates a set of waste disposal methods.

7. We treat our waste in accordance with the waste disposal methods set out by the government.

Words and phrases

waste 廢（棄）物	licensed 有執照的	treatment 處理
remove 搬開	hand tool 手工具	scrap 碎片
iron filings 鐵屑	recycling 回收	raw material 原料
reuse 再使用	effectively 有效地	amount 數量
protect 保護	regulate 管理	a set of 一組,一套
disposal 處理	method 方法	treat 處理
in accordance with 根據		

Dialogue

While the boss, Richard, is talking to Christine, he glances at the monitor screen accidentally and finds that an old woman is entering the factory area with a tricycle loaded with recyclables. Richard is annoyed and asks Lily to take care of this security vulnerability.

Richard: Why can this lady trespass onto our property so easily? Don't we have door access control?

Christine: Well, she lives nearby and is used to collecting recyclables from door to door. If the door is not closed, she will go in to take the waste she needs.

Richard: In order to ensure a safe working environment, employees should abide by the access control regulations. Or door access control will exist in name only.

Christine: Ok, I'll inform all employees to keep the door closed at all times.

Richard: By the way, how about the waste treatment? I was watching TV few days ago and learned that some thoughtless and selfish manufacturers illegally dumped of waste causing contamination to the river.

Christine: I heard that too. It's really awful. Contaminated water and soil will harm our health. Richard, you don't need to worry about it. We've cooperated with a waste clearance and treatment facility and they will come to collect the waste regularly.

Richard: Please also make sure employees recycle.

Christine: No problems with that. David is in charge of factory affairs and there is a good system of recycling in the factory.

Richard: Good. Now, let's get back to the topic.

The phone is ringing and Kate answers it.

Kate: Hi, this is Kate speaking. How can I help you?

Linda: Hi. This is Linda. May I speak to Lily, please?

Kate: Hold on a second. I'll put you through to her.

Lily: Lily speaking. Who's calling?

Linda: Hi, Lily. It's me, Linda. Do you have a minute? I need your help.

Lily: What's up?

Linda: A friend of mine asked me to find her a facility that can receive scrap iron. I'm wondering if your company does.

Lily: You've got the right person. I can give you the phone number of the facility that cooperates with us. They not only receive scrap iron and iron filings, but they also help us deal with unwanted products, such as goods that are no longer produced or rusted and defective products. They will remove the waste and pay for it. It's quite convenient for clearing up useless items.

Linda: Yes, it is. Thank you for such helpful information. I'll give my friend the phone number. By the way, are there any useless plastic items coming out of the manufacturing process in your factory?

Lily: Well, there are. We have small amounts of plastic waste. They are turned into small particles and used as recycling material. The products made out of it will have a lower price.

Linda: Do customers accept that kind of product? I think its quality may not be the same as the products made of the original raw materials.

Lily: We tell the customers honestly about the different quality of these two products before they place their order. Then they can make their own decision.

Linda: Ok. I've got it. Thank you very much for your time. I'll get back to work. Bye.

Lily: See you.

After hanging up the phone, Lily remembers that few days ago when she went to talk to David, she found that many obsolete items were stored in the warehouse for a while. In order to free more space to store the materials and goods to be shipped, she calls David for help.

Lily: Hi, David. This is Lily. I have a batch of goods to be shipped soon. And now I need some space to store them temporarily. Could you please free up space in the warehouse for the goods?

David: No problem. I'll take care of it.

Lily: Thank you, David. You are so kind.

Powerful word bank

glance 一瞥	monitor 顯示器	screen 螢幕
accidentally 意外地	tricycle 三輪腳踏車	recyclable 可回收物
annoy 惹惱	security 安全	vulnerability 弱點
trespass 擅自進入	collect 收集	exist 存在
thoughtless 欠考慮的	manufacturer 製造業者	illegally 非法地
dump 傾倒	contamination 汙染	awful 極糟的
soil 土壤	harm 傷害	facility 場所
unwanted 不需要的	rust 鐵鏽	useless 無用的
plastic 塑膠	particle 微粒	original 原始的
honestly 誠實地	decision 決定	obsolete 淘汰的
store 貯存	warehouse 倉庫	temporarily 臨時地

Useful phrases

door access control 門禁管制	from door to door 挨家挨戶地
abide by 遵守	in name only 表面上的；掛名的
What's up? 怎麼啦？	no longer 不再
clear up 清理	turn into 使變成
hang up 掛斷電話	for a while 一會兒
free up 騰出	

Discussion

1. What problems will be caused if a factory illegally discharges waste-water into the river?

2. If you found that someone was pouring waste into open space, what would you do?

 **MEMO**

UNIT 06 Endless Working Hours
無止盡的工作

Useful expressions

1. I have a heavy workload and wish I could be like an octopus to deal with so many different things at a time.

2. It's an eight-to-five job. I have a one-hour break for lunch.

3. I will take work home if I cannot finish it in the office.

4. I feel stressed because of the tense schedule of my duties.

5. I don't need to work on the weekends. But, if the packaging gets behind, I need to work overtime.

Words and phrases

endless 無休止的	workload 工作量	octopus 章魚
at a time 一次	stressed 感到有壓力的	tense 繃緊的
schedule 日程安排表	packaging 包裝（業）	get behind 落後
overtime 加班		

Dialogue

After a long weekend, many colleagues are busy with their work. While Lily is talking to her colleague about a new e-mail sent by a client, the phone rings.

Marie: Hello, this is Marie from the Sales Department. How may I help you?

Jenny: Hi, this is Jenny speaking. May I speak to Lily, please?

Marie: Hold on one second, please.

Lily: This is Lily.

Jenny: Hi, Lily. It's Jenny. I'd like to know if we can have dinner together this evening. We haven't gotten together for a long time.

Lily: That's a good idea. I'll give you a call when I finish work.

Jenny: All right. See you later.

When she hangs up the phone, Lily gets back to talk with her colleague.

Lily: A client has just placed a big order and has asked us to deliver it in a short time. Also, we have to prepare the products and ship them quickly. How are we going to manage it?

Vick: I think we need to work overtime this evening to help pack the goods.

Lily: Are you sure?

Vick: I'm afraid we have to and we may need more days to work on it. Do you think we can hire some casual laborers to help us?

Lily: I'll check with Human Resources. Unlike us, casual laborers will get hourly wages.

Vick: I was told that, although we work overtime, we might not get paid overtime because we are exempt employees who are not entitled to overtime pay.

Lily: So, we won't get paid overtime if we come in on the weekend. Are you sure?

Vick: Theoretically, yes. However, lately, many people have been talking about the policy of a five-day work week. According to the Labor Standards Act, when employees work overtime, the employer should pay overtime. They usually get paid time and a half for overtime.

Lily: Yes, I've heard about that. And I was told that many employers would not ask their employees to work overtime so that they could save manufacturing costs.

Vick: That's very interesting. The purpose of the new policy is to reduce working hours. As a result, workers can have more time with their families. Now, many of them are complaining to the government about the new policy because they have

PART **2**

fewer opportunities to work overtime and their income is relatively reduced.

Lily: Yeah, so the government, the labor unions and the corporate management still need to find an effective solution. After all, keeping a harmonious relation between employees and employers is very important.

Vick: No matter what happens, we still need to catch up to complete our work in time.

Lily: You're right. I need to call my friend to postpone our dinner.

Powerful word bank

place 開出（訂單）	deliver 運送	ship 運送
goods 貨物	hire 僱用	wage 薪水
entitle 給...權力（或資格）	theoretically 理論上	lately 最近
policy 政策	employer 雇主	purpose 目的
reduce 減少	government 政府	income 收入
relatively 相對地	effective 有效的	resolution 解決
harmonious 和諧的	relation 關係	complete 完成
postpone 使延期		

Useful phrases

hold on 不掛電話	get together 聚集
hang up 掛斷電話	casual laborer 臨時工
human resource 人力資源	exempt employee 責任制員工
according to 根據	Labor Standards Act 勞動基準法
manufacturing cost 製造成本	as a result 結果
labor unions 工會	after all 畢竟
catch up to 趕上	

Discussion

1. What do you think about the policy of a five-day work week?

2. What would you do if you could not complete your office work in time?

3. Which industries have long working hours?

4. Which do you prefer, long working hours with higher pay or normal working hours with lower pay? Why?

5. How do long working hours affect family time?

Supplementary information

Useful terms

one fixed day off and one flexible rest day 一例一休

five-day work week 一例一休

relation between labor and capital 勞資關係

the opposition between labor and capital 勞資對立

overtime 加班

employee 雇員

employer 雇主

overtime; overtime pay 加班費

hourly wage 時薪

time and a half 相當於實薪一倍半的加班費

double time 相當於實薪雙倍的加班費

UNIT 07 Telephone Manners
電話禮節

Useful expressions

1. Who would you like to speak to?

2. He/she is not in.

3. Would you like to leave a message?

4. Could you please take a message?

5. Could you ask him to call me back?

6. Please speak slowly.

7. Could you spell it?

8. I'm afraid you've got the wrong number.

Words and phrases

leave a message 留言　　take a message 留言　　call sb. back 回電

spell 拼寫

Dialogue

It's Kate's first day at work. She feels very nervous and worries that she may not handle matters appropriately. Lily is her supervisor and tries to ease her mind.

Kate: Good morning, Lily. Today is the first day at my new job and I hope you can direct me when I make mistakes.

Lily: Welcome. Don't worry. You'll be fine. Firstly, you need to know that you can't take too much time for personal telephone conversations during office hours. It's not allowed in our office rules.

Kate: Thank you for telling me that. I'll be sure to follow that rule. Do I need to answer the phone when it rings?

Lily: Sure. When the phone rings, please answer it immediately. There are many calls every day in our department. It's important to be patient when talking on the phone. Sometimes, foreign clients will call us directly. So I'd like to show you how to answer this kind of call.

Kate: It sounds intimidating. I'm not sure if I can handle it or not.

Lily: Don't worry. If you cannot understand the callers' intention, you can ask them to repeat. Of course, your tone needs to be very polite. For example, you can say, "I'm sorry. I didn't catch that. Could you repeat and say it slowly, please?"

Kate: If I still don't get it, what should I do?

Lily: I think you may tell the caller that you'll find someone to help you. Well, how about we practice the telephone conversation? I'll be a client.

Kate: This is interesting. Okay, let's start.

They are doing a telephone conversation role-play.

Kate: Hello, EZ Company. This is Kate speaking. How may I help you?

Lily: Hello, it is Lily from UCC Company. Is James there?

Kate: Please hold on a second. I'll put you through to the R&D Department.

Lily: Thank you very much. See, you did a good job. It's not that hard, right?

Kate: Thank you for your kindness. I'll try my best to complete my task.

At this moment, another call comes in. Kate answers the phone right away.

Kate: Hello, EZ company. This is Kate speaking. What can I do for you?

Louise: Hi, this is Louise. Is James there?

Kate: He just stepped out of the office to go to the Sales Department. Would you like to leave a message?

Louise: I'm sorry. I have a bad connection. I cannot hear you. I'll call you back.

Louise: It's Louise again. Can you put me through to the Sales Department, please?

Kate: Okay. If the line doesn't work, its extension is 2244.

Louise: Thank you very much.

Powerful word bank

appropriately 適當地	ease 使安心	direct 指點
personal 個人的	allow 允許	patient 有耐心的
directly 直接地	intimidating 令人膽怯的	intention 意圖
tone 語氣	task 任務	connection 連接
extension 電話分機		

Useful phrases

make a mistake 犯錯

office hours 上班時間

role play 角色扮演

put sb. through 把電話接過來

right away 立刻

Discussion

1. The phone is ringing and your co-workers are tired of answering it. You are the newcomer in this office. What would you do?

2. You are quite busy and have just finished an unpleasant conversation with your colleague. The phone rings. How will you answer?

3. If a foreign client asks you to take a message for your colleague, but you can't understand his accent, what would you do?

Supplementary information

Tips for a successful telephone conversation

· When the phone rings, pick it up right away.

· Use 'it is' to identify the person who is making the call and use 'this is' to identify the person who is answering the call. Don't use 'I am'.

· Speak politely, patiently, and attentively.

- Don't let the caller wait too long while putting him/her through to a specific office.

- If you are not sure what the caller said, ask him/her to repeat it and confirm the call.

- Ask if you can take a message.

UNIT 08 Migrant Workers 移工管理

Useful expressions

1. The migrant workers are from Vietnam mostly.

2. The human resources agency helps us recruit the migrant workers.

3. They work very hard.

4. Some of them can speak good Chinese.

5. After work, they like to play loud music in their living quarters.

Words and phrases

migrant worker 移工	Vietnam 越南	mostly 大多數地
human resources agency 人力銀行	recruit 徵募	living quarter 宿舍

Dialogue

Christin is a special assistant with the EZ Company. Today, she is leading a meeting to discuss two problems which have appeared in the company recently. One is the shortage of factory workers and the other is migrant worker recruitment.

Christin: Good morning, dear colleagues. Thank you for joining us at this meeting. There are two issues to discuss. As you know, we have received a big order recently and have to prepare a great number of goods in a short time. However, we have been suffering from a lack of manpower for many months. I hope you can give me some ideas to resolve the problems successfully.

David: Why not recruit middle-aged women in the neighborhood to join us? Their children have grown up and they may be willing to re-enter employment.

Christin: Thanks, David. Okay, I'll write that down – middle-aged women. Any other ideas?

James: Maybe we can cooperate with our neighboring factories by exchanging manpower. I mean, when they have some free hands and we have a shortage, they could give us some help without delay, and vice versa.

Lily: Hmm...I think that may cause some problems. For instance, the exchanged workers may not be familiar with our product requirements, or we'll all be working all the time so we won't be able to back each other up.

Christin: Yeah, that's a good point. What else? What do you think if we recruit more migrant workers since we've done it before?

David: In the long run, it may be a good idea. However, we were warned in the last inspection about the accommodation for migrant workers.

Christin: Don't worry about it. We've improved that part. Many of them are familiar with the manufacturing process in the factory. So, if we recruit anyone without experience, I think they can get support and adjust to their new life soon.

James: Great! I think you'd better take action as soon as possible. I don't want our shipping to get behind again.

After work, Lily goes to a restaurant to have dinner with her friend, Jenny.

Lily: Hi, Jenny. Sorry I'm late. I've been quite busy recently. How are you doing?

Jenny: Same as you. I'm glad that we can finally get together. I'm starving. Let's get something to eat first.

Waitress: Are you ready to order?

Lily: Yes. May I have a vegetarian hot pot and an ice cream for dessert?

Waitress: Yes of course. And how about you, Miss?

Jenny: I'd like to have a hot pot with beef. And I'll go with lemon juice.

Waitress: Okay, let me confirm your order. One vegetarian hot pot and ice cream. One hot pot with beef and lemon juice. Is that all?

Lily: Yes.

Waitress: Would you like the dessert and drink together with the main course or after it?

Jenny: After the meal will be fine. Thank you. So, what are you busy with these days?

Lily: I have to help the Packaging Department with a large quantity of merchandise that a client has ordered. There is a shortage of manpower in my company.

Jenny: Interesting. A similar situation is also happening in my company. And now we're recruiting a group of migrant workers.

Lily: Where are they from? And how are you arranging their room and board? My company is going to do it, too.

Jenny: An agent will help us look for the workers. They're from Vietnam, Thailand, and Indonesia. Before they come to Taiwan, they have to learn basic Chinese. The company has staff quarters for them to stay in. On weekdays, the company will order lunch boxes for them. After work, they can cook for themselves. There's a kitchen in their living place.

Lily: How do you communicate with them? They are from different countries and their Chinese may not be good enough.

Jenny: Language is not a big problem. We have interpreters who can speak Vietnamese and Thai. And their people who are already here will help them, too. In addition, when they first arrive at the factory, they will be informed of compulsory requirements, such as quality control, required work overtime, following regulations, required performance on work, and environment maintenance. They usually follow the rules. Of course, we also pay attention to their living and physical situations. We hope that they can adjust their life well and work with us easily.

Lily: Do you know what they do to kill time when they are free?

Jenny: They used to work overtime frequently so that they could make more money. Since the new policy launched, they seldom work overtime and will stay in their living place to listen to music or cook together.

Lily: Thank you for giving me so much helpful information. I'll share it with my colleagues. Hmmm...the ice cream tastes great.

Powerful word bank

appear 出現	recently 最近	shortage 缺少
issue 問題	manpower 人力	middle-aged 中年的
neighborhood 鄰近地區	exchange 交換	delay 耽擱
cause 使發生	requirement 必要條件	warn 警告

accommodation 住處	support 支持	adjust 調整
vegetarian 吃素的	confirm 確認	Thailand 泰國
Indonesia 印尼	interpreter 口譯員	compulsory 必須做的
regulation 規定	performance 成果	maintenance 維持
physical 身體的	frequently 頻繁地	launch 發出

Useful phrases

special assistant 特別助理	a number of 一些
suffer from 受...困擾	be willing to 願意
vice versa 反之亦然	for instance 例如
be familiar with 熟悉	back up 支持
in the long run 從長遠來看	take action 採取行動
hot pot 火鍋	main course 主菜
quantity of 大量	room and board 食宿
staff quarter 員工宿舍	lunch box 便當
quality control 品質控制	pay attention to 關心
kill time 打發時間	used to 過去經常

Discussion

1. How many migrant workers come to Taiwan to work annually?

2. Which countries do those workers come from?

3. What do you think is an effective way of migrant worker management?

4. If you find a migrant worker encounters problems on the street, what would you do?

MEMO

UNIT 09 Help Wanted 徵才

Useful expressions

1. Conventional industry has been suffering from a lack of manpower for a long time.

2. Young people prefer to work in service rather than in conventional industry nowadays.

3. A well-organized resume is essential for looking for a job.

4. What we expect of the newcomers is their work attitudes.

5. Appropriate manners for job seekers, such as being punctual, being polite, dressing formally, and smiling, are basic requirements.

6. Recruiting students as interns may be a way of resolving the shortage of manpower.

Words and phrases

conventional 傳統式的	industry 行業	prefer 寧願（選擇）
rather than 而不是...	nowadays 現今	resume 履歷表
essential 必要的	attitude 態度	punctual 準時的
formally 正式地	intern 實習生	

Dialogue

Certain departments – accounting, sales, and research and development (R&D) – are eager for new employees. Therefore, the human resource office is recruiting new working partners. The director, Mr. Tu is asking his coworkers for their opinions.

Mr. Tu: We are going to recruit new employees to join us. Do you know anybody who is looking for a job and can take an active part in running the business?

Louise: One of my friends just quit his job last month and is looking for a new job now.

Mr. Tu: Why did he quit his job? How's his work performance?

Louise: He told me that he felt tired of working in the hi-tech industry. The working hours are quite long and he often felt exhausted and stressed. And he was once awarded the Employee of the Year award at work. He works really hard and I think his performance is quite good.

Mr. Tu: What is his educational background? Does he know how to operate specific computer programs?

Louise: He majored in Industrial Engineering and Management at school and has worked in the relevant industry for six years. His previous job was related to computer operations. So I think he should have no problem with it.

Mr. Tu: Can you ask him to send a resume to us?

Louise: Okay, I'll tell him later.

Jennifer: I'm wondering how we'll know that the job seekers aren't exaggerating their work competency in their resumes.

Lily: Ha...I had this experience once. I'd like to share it with you. In the Sales Department, we use the program, Microsoft Office, to do business frequently. So, once, I gave a job seeker a sample copy and asked her to create a similar one using Microsoft Office. She failed although she had indicated in her resume that she had learned that computer skill and had gotten a good grade at school. We have no time to teach the newcomers how to use computer programs. We expect that they can start to work on their first day. So, I think it's a good way to give the job seekers a quiz before hiring them.

Mr. Tu: That's very interesting. So, Louise will help find one person to fill the position in the R&D Department. We still need an accounting assistant.

Jennifer: We can post help wanted ads on our website and classified ads in the newspaper.

Mr. Tu: Thank you all for giving me so many good ideas. I'll ask my assistant to make up the ads as soon as possible.

Louise: May I ask a question?

Mr. Tu: Yes, go ahead.

Louise: I'll call my friend and ask him to send us his resume right away. But he may ask me about the salary. Since he has worked for many years, will the company take his previous work experience into consideration?

Mr. Tu: When we receive his resume, we'll see about that. As you know, we follow the official regulations and I think your friend can understand that.

Louise: Okay, I'll tell him. Thank you very much.

Mr. Tu: By the way, Jennifer, could you please browse through all the resumes to make sure they conform to the basic requirements.

Jennifer: No problem. I'll collect all the qualified application forms and put them on your desk.

Mr. Tu: Thanks a lot. I hope we can get the right man to join our team.

Powerful word bank

certain 某一	accounting 會計	therefore 因此
director 主管	coworker 同事	quit 停止
hi-tech 高科技	exhaust 使精疲力盡	award 授予
operate 運作	specific 特定的	program 程式
major 主修	exaggerate 誇大	competency 能力

similar 類似的	indicate 指出	grade 成績
position 職務	salary 薪水	browse 瀏覽
collect 收集	qualified 合格的	obtain 獲得

Useful phrases

eager for 渴望	Industrial Engineering and Management 工業工程與管理
relate to 與...有關	classified ads 分類廣告
make up 給...排版	take sth. into consideration 考慮到
conform to 符合	application form 申請表

Discussion

1. What basic conditions are young graduates required to have when they are trying to get employment?

2. What educational backgrounds do graduates need to find a job in conventional industry?

3. Why do many young people prefer to work in service rather than in conventional industry?

Supplementary information

Tips for the resume

- Items contain: job objective, education, awards, work experience, languages, interests, key skills, certificates, and positions and responsibilities. If the job seekers have no performance in certain areas, those items can be optional.

- State your job objective clearly.

- Keep descriptions short, clear, and concise.

- The format needs to look neat and organized.

Job seekers etiquette

- Dress formally. Sandals and flip-flops are not allowed.

- If an accident occurs and you cannot make the interview in time, call in advance.

- Keep smiling.

- Do not play on a smartphone while waiting for the interview.

- No food and drink.

Tips for being qualified interns

Many conventional industries have built up internship programs with technological universities. How to be the intern today and become the employee tomorrow:

- Work seriously on the task assigned.

- Actively take the designated job.

- Get along well with co-workers.

- Find questions and problems in the work and try to resolve them.

- Enjoy learning and take challenges as a new mission.

- Don't be too fussy about small details.

- Take extra jobs as training and learning.

- Ask for help if you don't know how to do it.

 **MEMO**

UNIT 10 In-service Training Program 員工在職訓練

Useful expressions

1. Sometimes, I'll take a free class, like English, in the company after I finish my work.

2. I hope the company can offer us Japanese classes because I would like to take a trip to Japan during annual leave.

3. Some training programs are compulsory. Every employee is required to take them.

4. Many of us cannot take the training programs because we need to go home directly after work to take care of our children.

5. We can learn some practical skills from the training program.

6. Sometimes, the special assistant will ask us what skills we would like to learn before she applies for the programs granted by the government.

Words and phrases

offer 提供	take a trip 旅行	after work 下班
take care of 處理	practical 實用的	apply for 申請
grant 准予		

PART **②**

Dialogue

Lately, EZ company has recruited many new employees who are graduating from college or just finishing military service. The Human Resource office is planning to arrange relevant training programs for the newcomers.

Mr. Tu: Kelly, could you help arrange some programs for the newcomers? Also, please ask the relevant supervisors to join the programs as well.

Kelly: Ok, when should we make the offer of programs? During working hours, after work, or on weekends?

Mr. Tu: I think after work will be better so that work progress will not be delayed. What programs are you thinking of providing?

Kelly: How about a seminar related to work place safety? I'll invite an experienced speaker to give our colleagues a three-hour talk with actual cases.

Mr. Tu: That's great. I hope that the newcomers will fit in quickly and get familiar with their new job. I don't want it to happen again that the new employees are not familiar with their tasks and do not perform satisfactorily resulting in a follow-up affair delay.

Christine: Hope it doesn't happen again. So, that's why you'd like to ask their supervisors to attend the programs, right? If an employee who is in charge of a certain business quits halfway through, the supervisors can find an appropriate person to take up the post right away. By the way, it's time to have a fire drill again.

Mr. Tu: Thank you for reminding me. Everything just follows the same practice. Announce this information to all departments and let them know when and where to do it. Ask them to assign people who haven't participated in this event to participate in the drill. Fire drills are compulsory for everyone in this company.

Christine: By the way, the proposals granted by the government have been approved. Do I need to announce this information to the public too?

Mr. Tu: Certainly. Why not post the information on the bulletin board and remind them via e-mail to read it?

Christine: Ok, I'll do that now. Everybody will be busy again.

During the lunch break, James, Lily, and Penny are having their lunch together and talking about the programs granted by the government.

Lily: Three programs are going to be offered in the company soon. Have you decided which program you're interested in joining, James?

James: I took a 3D printing program last time and I wish they could offer an advanced class this time, but they can't.

Lily: Why would you like to take an advanced class? Isn't the previous program enough for you to deal with your work?

James: In the R&D department, I need to design and create new products and modify some unsatisfactory products with the machine. The equipment is programmed so I need to learn how to use it skillfully. How about you?

Lily: I've taken the English program since it started a year ago and I'm glad it will be offered again. There are two levels provided and I'm going to take the intermediate level. Why not join me, James? How about you, Penny?

James: Hmmm…let me think about it. I'll get back to you.

Penny: I haven't had a chance to learn English since I graduated from college. I'm interested in English a lot. I'll sign up for the basic class.

Lily: When will those classes start?

Penny: They will start next month. All of them are offered in the evening after work. Also, each class will have a three-hour meeting once a week and they will run for three months.

James: Do we have to pay and are there any quizzes?

Lily: They are all free. I'm not sure if there're any quizzes or not. We should check with the instructors later.

James: Where do we go to take the classes?

Lily: It's very convenient because we just stay in the company and the instructors come to us.

Penny: So, that's one benefit for the employees. But, I think it will be very tiring to take the classes after working all day long.

Lily: I think so. Well, no pain, no gain. Let's just go for it.

Powerful word bank

seminar 討論會	experienced 有經驗的	talk 演講
actual 實際的	perform 執行	Satisfactorily 令人滿意地
follow-up 採取進一步行動	affair 業務	quit 辭職
announce 發布	assign 指定	participate 參加
proposal 提案	approve 批准	via 經由
advanced 高級的	modify 修改	level 程度
intermediate 中級的	quiz 測驗	convenient 方便的
tiring 令人疲倦的		

Useful phrases

graduate from 從…畢業	military service 兵役
work progress 工作進展	fit in 使適應
get familiar with 熟悉	result in 導致
halfway through …到一半時	take up the post 出任
right away 立刻	fire drill 消防演習
the public 公眾	bulletin board 布告欄
sign up 報名登記	no pain, no gain 一分耕耘，一分收穫

Discussion

1. What's the purpose of the newcomers taking the relevant training programs?

2. Is it necessary for the enterprise to hold training programs for their employees?

Supplementary information

The government encourages and provides grants for enterprises to hold training programs for their employees in Taiwan. Based on their needs, an enterprise will plan several training programs at a time. The contents of the programs may include:

- ERP training　Enterprise Resource Planning 企業資源規劃。就是企業通過數據紀錄和分析，持續改進自身經營方法。

- Lean Production Training　精實生產訓練。就是希望將一家公司的企業經營成沒有任何資源浪費的現象，使能創造更多利潤並永續成長。

- 3D printing skills　學習使用 3D 設計、繪圖、及印製成品的技巧。

- Language programs　外語學習課程。提升員工外語能力，讓企業走向國際化。

　In order to improve employees' competency, sometimes the employer will pay for the programs. It's a type of benefit for the employees as well.

MEMO

職場英文
English for Specific Workplace

<table>
<tr><td>UNIT
11</td><td>Product Design and
Manufacturing
產品設計與製造</td></tr>
</table>

Useful expressions

1. The R&D department can customize the products according to the buyers' needs.

2. When the boss found something new, he would ask us to try to design a similar one.

3. In order to inspire more ideas for creating new products, the boss will visit international hardware shows and share his findings with us.

4. We have to learn the new software in order to know how to make the specific products.

5. In addition to creating and developing new products, we also need to provide administrative support when necessary.

Words and phrases

customize 訂做	according to 根據	buyer 買主
inspire 激勵	hardware 五金器具；硬體	software 軟體
specific 具體的	administrative support 行政上的支援	

Dialogue

A client called James yesterday that the sample product developed by his department, R&D, did not meet the client's need. So, this morning James went to visit this client specifically to find out what he could do. James is one hour late to the office today.

Lily: You're late for work. Where have you been?

James: I just got back from a client's office. He's not satisfied with the item we designed.

Lily: How did you deal with this problem with him?

James: Well, we examined the object which was made at the client' request. It does not conform 100% to the client's need. However, we talked for a little while and he realized its effect and accepted our explanation.

Lily: Great. Your job is very challenging, isn't it? You need to design and develop objects that are requested by our clients. Have you ever encountered any difficulties or problems in the process of making new products?

James: Yes. When that happens, I'll ask my supervisor to give me advice. Or, I'll ask our boss or the client to have a meeting so I can find a way to resolve the problem. And I always make the product.

Lily: You are very smart and responsible. I'm curious to know how you create an item going from zero to a full, concrete object?

James: The client will propose his/her idea, provide a sample product, or give a direction to us. Then, we make a proof assisted by 3D printing machine and manufacture the specific product once the sample is confirmed by the client.

Lily: So, people in your department all need to know how to operate specific computer programs so that they can be competent at work.

James: That's right. Lately, we've been recruiting new employees because one guy just quit and another guy intends to quit too.

Lily: How does one become a qualified employee in your department? Do they need any skills? Or, will you give them training after they join the company?

James: It's a very busy department and we have no extra time to give newcomers training. So, a qualified employee must be aware of using two basic computer programs, Auto Cad and Solid Works, before they can join our team. In addition to the 3D plotter machine, we also have a torque-testing machine. We show the newcomers how to use them whenever colleagues need help.

Lily: So, most of the time, you focus on your portion of the work, right? But, I found you also help colleagues from other departments. How come? You've been so busy.

James: Sometimes, when I'm available and someone needs my help, I'll go to help him/her. Like yesterday, I missed a phone call from my friend because I was asked to go to get a batch of goods with a colleague.

Lily: The supplier should deliver the goods directly to us, shouldn't he?

James: Yes, but we can't wait for the shipment. Our customer is expecting the goods urgently. So we need to go get them in person and pack them in our factory before shipping them, or, we'll fall behind. I'm just like a lifeguard who goes to help people who are in hot water.

Lily: You are such a good guy. No wonder you are so popular in the company.

James: No way! However, I'm going to have to pass on this job to someone else since there are more and more issues to take care of in my department and one guy is leaving now.

Lily: Well, I think you'd help people again if they begged you.

Powerful word bank

sample 樣本	specifically 特別地	effect 效果
explanation 說明	responsible 認真負責的	curious 渴望知道的
concrete 具體的	propose 提出	proof 樣張

competent 有能力的	extra 額外的	portion 部分
supplier 供應商	urgently 緊急地	lifeguard 救生員
beg 懇求		

Useful Phrases

meet sb's need 符合某人的需要	find out 發現
be aware of 意識到	torque-testing 扭轉力測試
a batch of 一組；一群；一批	fall behind 落後
in hot water 有麻煩	No way! 當然不
pass on 傳遞	

Discussion

1. In addition to the computer program, what materials do designers need to create a concrete object with the 3D plotter?

2. If you are intending to make an action figure with the 3D plotter, what character would you like to make and why?

Supplementary information

常見英文縮寫解析

AED	Automated External Defibrillators 自動體外心臟去顫器
AI	Artificial Intelligence 人工智慧
APEC	Asia-Pacific Economic Cooperation 亞太經合組織
ASAP	as soon as possible 盡快
ATM	automated/ automatic teller machine 自動櫃員機
BOT 模式	Build, Operate, Transfer 民間興建營運後轉移模式
BTW	by the way 順帶一提
CCTV	Closed-Circuit Television 閉路電視
CEO	**Chief Executive Officer 首席執行長**
CIF	COST, INSURANCE, FREIGHT 成本加保險費加運費
CNC	Computer Numerical Control 電腦數值控制
DINK	Double Income, No Kids 雙薪，無子女
DIY	Do It Yourself 自己動手製作
ECFA	Cross-Straits Economic Cooperation Framework Agreement 兩岸經濟合作架構協議
e.g.	For example 例如；舉例來說
FOB	Free On Board 離岸價
FTA	Free Trade Agreement 自由貿易協定

FYI	For Your Information 供您參考
GDP	Gross Domestic Product 國內生產總值
HR	**Human Resources 人力資源**
i.e.	that is 亦即；也就是說
IE	Internet Explorer 網頁瀏覽器
IoT	Internet of Things 物聯網
IT	Information Technology 資訊科技
KPI	Key Performance Indicators 關鍵績效指標
LOL	laugh out loud 大聲笑
MICE	Meetings, Incentives, Conferencing/ Conventions, Exhibitions/ Exposition 會議、獎勵旅遊、大型企業會議、活動展覽
MOE	Ministry of Education 教育部
MRT	Mass Rapid Transit 大眾捷運系統
OEM	Original Equipment Manufacturer 代工生產
OOO	**Out Of Office 不在辦公室**
PDCA	Plan-Do-Check-Act 規劃、執行、查核、行動
PM	**Project Manager 專案經理**
PO	Purchase order 訂單
PR	**Public Relations 公共關係**
p.s.	post script 附註或說明（只限用在書信中）

QA	Quality Assurance 品質保證
ROTC	Reserved Officers Training Corps 預備軍官訓練團
RSVP	please reply 請回覆
SKU	Stock Keeping Unit 庫存量單位
SOHO	Small Office Home Office 在家辦公
SOP	Standard Operation Procedure 標準作業程序
SWOT	AnalysisStrength, Weakness, Opportunity, Threat 強弱危機分析
TBA	**To Be Announced 待公佈**
TPP	**Trans-Pacific Partnership 跨太平洋夥伴協定**
TTYL	Talk To You Later 晚點聊
UN	United Nations 聯合國
USR	University Social Responsibility 大學社會責任
WHO	World Health Organization 世界衛生組織
WTO	World Trade Organization 世界貿易組織

PART **②**

UNIT 12 Employee Welfare 員工福利

Useful expressions

1. We are a stable systematic company.

2. All regulations set in this company conform to the Labor Standard Act.

3. The full-time workers are entitled to take the benefits set by the government.

4. We are given incentive payments three times a year.

5. We work five days a week and have weekends off.

6. The biggest benefit given by the company is annual incentive travel.

7. The company covers all travel expenses for its employees.

8. Does your company provide parental leave?

Words and phrases

stable 平穩的	systematic 有系統的	benefit 好處
incentive payment 獎勵津貼	annual 一年一次的	incentive travel 獎勵旅遊
expense 費用	parental leave 育嬰假	

Dialogue

James has been working at the EZ Company for four and a half years. He has been suffering from stomach upset for months and his doctor suggests that he'd better take a leave of absence for two months.

Lily: Hi, James. You look pale. Are you okay?

James: No. I feel sick and need to see a doctor. Can you help me request a sick leave?

Lily: Sure, no problem. Do you need a ride to the clinic?

James: I can go myself. Thank you very much.

Lily: Are you sure?

James: Yes, I'm sure.

A week later, James goes to the Human Resource office and talks to the director.

James: Good morning, Mr. Tu. I'm afraid that I have to take a two-month leave of absence on the advice of my doctor.

Mr. Tu: What's wrong? I've heard that you are not very well lately.

James: I've been suffering from stomach upset for months and the doctor suggested that I should be away from my current job for a while. Here's the medical certificate.

ABC 職場英文
English for Specific Workplace

Mr. Tu: I'm sorry to hear about that. In addition to leave of absence, you also can take annual leave. I hope you can recover your health and come back soon.

James: Thanks. I will.

The EZ Company is going to hold an annual outing for their employees. Christin is leading a meeting with the representatives from individual departments.

Christin: Time flies very fast. The annual outing is coming up again. So, where would everyone like to go to this year?

Fanny: Can we go to Hualian? They have beautiful scenery and an exciting outdoor activity – whitewater rafting. I've been looking forward to visiting for a long time.

Lily: Whitewater rafting! No way. It's very scary. I did it once and almost had an accident. To me, it's a very scary and dangerous activity. Why not Penghu? There is a beautiful beach and we can play water games as well.

Christin: I agree with Lily on the trip to Penghu. Although I've been there once with my friends, I'd like to visit it again. We can also go there on a cruise and come back by air.

Penny: That's a very good idea. It will be high season and we may need to book the tickets in advance. Can we bring our family with us?

Christin: Yes, families welcome to join us. The event will be free of charge for employees. Having a free outing is one of the benefits we have. However, family members need to pay: for each adult it's NT$1,500, and children under 12, NT$500.

Lily: That's great. It's a shame that Jennifer cannot join us this time. She is going to take maternity leave. And she's going to take parental leave after that.

Henry: So, this means that we won't see her for a while. Same with James. He is taking leave without pay to care for a physical problem. I hope Jennifer and James can join us next year.

Powerful word bank

pale 蒼白的	clinic 診所	recover 恢復
outing 短途旅遊	individual 個人的	scenery 風景
scary 可怕的	cruise（坐船）旅行	book 預訂
charge 索價		

Useful phrases

stomach upset 腸胃不適	had better 最好
leave of absence 請假	sick leave 病假
Human Resource office 人資室	medical certificate 醫療證書
annual leave 年休假	whitewater rafting 泛舟
look forward to 期待	as well 也
by air 乘飛機	high season 旺季
in advance 預先	It's a shame. 真是可惜
maternity leave 產假	leave without pay 留職停薪

Discussion

1. Which company gives their employees more benefits than other companies in Taiwan?

2. What is a sweatshop?

3. In general, how much time do employees get for parental leave? Do male and female employees have equal treatment?

Supplementary information

Employee benefits package

labor insurance 勞保	health insurance 健保
reward system 獎勵制度	promotion system 升遷制度
pension plan 退休制度	leave without pay 留職停薪
maternity leave 產假	parental leave 育嬰假
paternity leave 陪產假	take a leave of absence 請假
paid leave 有薪假	unpaid leave 無薪假
paid time off 帶薪休假	personal leave 事假
sick leave 病假	business leave 公假
annual leave 年假	

UNIT 13

Annual Incentive Travel
員工旅遊

Useful expressions

1. Incentive travel always gives employees wonderful memories.

2. The photos posted on the wall in the reception room were taken during our previous travels.

3. Everybody on the trip seems to be relieved from their stress at work.

4. Most colleagues like to bring their family to join the annual big event and meet other people.

5. After the trip, the distance between colleagues is less. And the working atmosphere becomes more relaxed and fun.

6. We usually hold the travel in the springtime. The weather is more comfortable than in other seasons.

Words and phrases

relief 慰藉	stress 壓力	distance 距離
atmosphere 氣氛	springtime 春天	

Dialogue

EZ Company holds the outing to Penghu over the long weekend and it is a three-day tour. Everyone is very excited. Many employees take their family with them. After the three-day tour, although everyone is exhausted, they feel relaxed and it seems that the distance between coworkers is decreasing. This is the main purpose of the employer holding the tour and, fortunately, it has reached the expected goal. Lily tells her friend what they did on the tour.

Lily: Wow, the tour was really tiring but we had a great time. Our boss is very generous. He spent a lot of money sponsoring this activity.

Alice: Who was in charge of this tour? And what did you do in *Penghu*?

Lily: All the activities were organized by a travel agency. They are very experienced in holding such kinds of company outings. For three days they provided many interesting activities and games for us to do.

Alice: There are many small offshore islands in *Penghu*. Did you visit all of them?

Lily: Of course not. We just visited the two main islands by ferry and tour bus. Here are the photos taken there.

Alice: What are the most exciting activities you did there?

Lily: Well, we went snorkeling, fed seagulls, and had an ecology tour during the day.

Alice: What do you mean 'ecology tour'?

Lily: The tour guide took us to an intertidal zone and showed us its unique ecology.

Alice: What else did you do there?

Lily: We had a barbecue for dinner and went fishing on a boat.

Alice: Who prepared the food for the barbecue?

Lily: The travel agent prepared everything for us.

Alice: How did you go fishing? You brought a fishing rod with you?

Lily: No. It's very interesting. There were many fishing rods sitting on both sides of the fishing boat. We just sat and waited for the fish to take the bait.

Alice: That sounds really fun. Did you catch any fish?

Lily: I don't remember because when we were fishing, there were fireworks shows in the dark sky. It was gorgeous.

Alice: Really? Who paid for it?

Lily: The boss. People said that he spent about fifty thousand dollars on a three-minute fireworks show.

Alice: He is very kind to try to please you guys.

Lily: He really is. Many of us appreciate what he's done for us. Yes, I've had a great break and have fully recharged for work again. And I'm looking forward to next year's trip.

Alice: Lucky you!

Powerful word bank

main 主要的	fortunately 幸運地	reach 達到
goal 目標	generous 慷慨的	sponsor 贊助
experienced 有經驗的	offshore 離岸的	island 島嶼
ferry 渡輪	seagull 海鷗	ecology 生態
unique 獨特的	bait 誘餌	firework 煙火
gorgeous 華麗的	please 討好	appreciate 感激
recharge 再充電		

Useful phrases

in charge of 負責	travel agency 旅行社
tour bus 遊覽車	go snorkeling 浮潛
intertidal zone 潮間帶	have a barbecue 烤肉
go fishing 釣魚	fishing rod 釣竿
fishing boat 漁船	Lucky you! 你真幸運！

Discussion

1. What are the advantages for a company to hold an incentive travel for employees?

2. In addition to the incentive travel, what else would big corporations provide for their employees?

3. If you were the activity planner, what activities would you like to provide for the incentive travel?

 **MEMO**

UNIT 14 Negotiating a Better Price through Email 議價商業書信

Useful expressions

1. The cost keeps increasing. I need to send e-mails to keep our clients informed.

2. Thank you very much for your swift reply.

3. Please accept my heartfelt apologies for the delay.

4. Please send my best regards to your family.

5. Please stay in touch.

6. I'm looking forward to hearing from you soon.

7. Thank you for your cooperation.

Words and phrases

swift 迅速的	reply 答覆	accept 接受
heartfelt 衷心的	apology 道歉	regards 關心
stay in touch 與...保持聯繫		

Dialogue

Lily is the director of the Sales Department. One of her jobs is to deal with foreign clients by e-mail. Due to the continuous rising costs of raw material and manpower, Lily has to send a price increase notice to her client. Negotiating a better price between the two parties starts.

Dear Lily,

The price should be good enough for me to increase your PO* volume. We will be adjusting the buying plan in 1~2 weeks after all quotes are finished, and we will start sending you more orders next month.

Thank you for your cooperation!

Best regards,

Jim

---

*PO: purchase order 訂貨（單）

In the previous mail, the buyer promised that he would place more orders. However, Lily didn't receive a follow-up e-mail so she is sending an e-mail to confirm the deal.

Dear Jim,

The price has been lowered as you requested. Also, you indicated that you would start sending more orders in February. However, the last order – number 37380-6319043 – sent by your company was placed on January 27th. Since then, we haven't received any new orders. Under these circumstances, I'm afraid that we cannot afford to pay the high insurance. Our insurance is going to expire on March 30th. If you have good price, please reconfirm your quantity of inventory and place more orders.

Thank you very much.

Best wishes,
Lily

Because of the rising costs, Lily informs her client the reason for increasing prices.

Dear Jack,

Thank you very much for your satisfaction with our products over the years. Your kind support inspires us to make progress constantly. We greatly appreciate it.

Because of the increasing price of steel materials since the 3rd and 4th quarters, (up to 15%,) cost of materials keeps increasing which causes our production costs to rise up to 7~8%. Moreover, a new Labor Standards Act implemented in 2017, the strict five-day work regulation, leads to higher personnel and processing costs. Plastic and paper manufacturers have increased their product prices as well. In these circumstances, we need to increase our selling price by 3%. The new price will be applied on orders effective May 1st, 2017.

Sincerely,

Lily

After receiving the note on price increase, the foreign client tries to negotiate a better deal with Lily.

Dear Lily,

I understand. However, I should inform you that this has been a difficult time of intense price competition in tool retailing in the U.S. Now that we have over 750 stores, we are taking market shares from every tool retailer, and they are attacking on all sides with lower pricing to try to win back their customers. To maintain our growth, we had to lower prices and offer more discounts and promotions than ever before to compete. I highly encourage you to hold pricing as long as possible for our SKU* because low prices are our strength in the market and prices are what keep us growing. We gave you more business this year because of a mistake from your competitor – if you can hold pricing, then we can continue giving you a higher PO volume permanently.

Kind regards,
Jack

---

*SKU: stock keeping unit 庫存量

When Lily received the e-mail, she replied to her client and tried to make him understand her difficulty.

Dear Jack,

Thank you very much for your reply. I'm afraid that we cannot hold pricing as you wish. We really cannot bear the price increase on raw materials, processing costs and the current exchange rate fluctuations. We have no choice but to slightly increase the price by 3%. In fact, we have tried everything to bear the price increase as much as possible. I hope you can understand our difficulties.

I'm looking forward to hearing from you soon.
Lily

However, the client still tries to cut the price. In order to maintain the business relationship with this client, Lily has to compromise and asks her assistant to make a calculation to give a final price.

Dear Jack,

Thank you very much for the order. However, I need to claim sincerely that the unit cost you set is much lower than our expected price. I've checked the price carefully and the final unit cost I can offer is 8.87, instead of 8.71. This is only a 1.8% increase to the original price. Please understand our difficulty and thank you very much for the business.

Sincerely,

Lily

Powerful word bank

negotiate 協商	volume （生產，交易等的）量	quote 報價
promise 承諾	follow-up 後續的	deal 交易
circumstance 情況	afford 支付得起	insurance 保險
expire 到期	inventory 存貨	satisfaction 滿意
inspire 激勵	constantly 不斷地	steel 鋼

quarter 季	implement 實施	strict 嚴格的
personnel 員工	processing 加工	plastic 塑膠
competition 競爭	retail 零售	attack 攻擊
discount 折扣	promotion 促銷	encourage 鼓勵
strength 實力	competitor 競爭者	permanently 永久地
fluctuation 波動	slightly 稍微地	compromise 妥協
calculation 計算結果	final 最後的	claim 聲稱
sincerely 誠懇地		

Useful phrases

due to 由於	raw material 原料
make progress 進展	lead to 導致...後果
market share 市場占有率	ever before 以前
bear the price 承擔價格	exchange rate 外匯率
in fact 事實上	unit cost 單位成本
original price 原價	

Discussion

1. If your client insists on maintaining the price while the cost of the raw materials keeps growing, what would you do?

2. It is normal to have price competition between peer trades in the market and may cause unpleasant outcome. If you were one of them, how can you create a win-win situation?

Supplementary information

Tips for writing a business e-mail

1. Note the subject of the message first so that it is easy to identify the purpose of individual emails afterwards.

2. It's not necessary to add the date at the top of the mail. The system will do it automatically.

3. In the message body, start with 'Dear' and then an official title before the last name of the addressee.

4. In the negotiation letter, the tone of the message needs to be polite but firm.

5. In the closing, add a salutation, such as regards, sincerely, and cordially.

6. Put the sender's name under the salutation.

Useful terms

supplier 供應商   manufacturer 製造商

PO (purchase order) 訂單   contract 合約

damage 損壞   shortage 數量短缺

complaint 抱怨   payment 付款

T/T (telegraphic transfer) 電匯   negotiating a better price 訂單議價

Payment: T/T 30% before production, and T/T 70% within 14 days after shipment.

付款方式：生產前先電匯 30%訂金，出貨後 14 天內電匯 70%尾款。

forging delay 鍛品延誤   manufacturing process 製造過程

deferred shipment 延期出貨

 **MEMO**

UNIT 15

Effective Interdepartmental Communication
部門之間的有效溝通

Useful expressions

1. We have communication problems between different departments.

2. We need to improve communication skills.

3. A good workplace ethic can keep the company achieving its goal.

4. Poor communication hinders implementation of work policies.

5. Strong interpersonal relationships make a successful team.

6. A harmonious working environment leads to good work performance.

7. Different opinions and conflicts appearing in the workplace are natural. That is what effective communication skills are for.

Words and phrases

workplace ethic 職場倫理	achieve 實現	hinder 阻礙
implementation 實踐	interpersonal relationship 人際關係	
conflict 衝突	natural 自然的	

Dialogue

Lately, many workers have been constantly complaining about the endless amount of work as well as work overtime. In the meantime, the owner of EZ Company, Richard, finds that coordination between departments seems ineffective and leads to misunderstanding. In order to lift office morale, Richard decides to hold an interim meeting at the lunch hour so that employees can have lunch together and share their opinions with one another.

Richard: Christin, could you inform the directors of each department to attend the interim meeting at noon in the conference room. And please order lunch boxes for the attendees. I'm going to lead the meeting in person today.

Christin: All right. I'll do it right away.

At the meeting...

Richard: Thank you for coming, dear partners. The purpose of this meeting is to find a way to resolve a recent problem. I found that implementation of work policies is not like it used to be. Please be aware: we are a team. Thus, if one part goes wrong, it will affect the overall situation. Now, please feel free to have your lunch and also to propose your valuable opinions.

Lily: The implementation of work policies is declining because we have too much work to deal with at a time so we cannot complete it in time.

James: We are facing difficulties in communicating with some departments. Some colleagues have unfriendly manners when we need their help.

Henry: My department doesn't dare take too many orders because we're afraid that we may not finish our products and ship them to the customers on time.

Lily: That reminds me. I've been encountering a serious problem lately when it's time to ship our goods. It seems that the Department of Production Management doesn't regularly conduct the required examination of their warehouses, for example, the inventory of raw materials and goods. I need to postpone the shipping date because of the shortage goods in stock.

Richard: Thank you very much for your constructive opinions. It's great that we are aware what problems we are facing. Now, what we need to do is to find resolutions. I think one problem we need to take care of is to improve communication skills. I believe efficient communication will make work easier.

James: Yes, you are right. I think the unfriendly situation I encountered may be because I didn't express my intentions clearly.

Lily: And because of insufficient communication skills, it's hard for us to convey our thinking in words to each other.

Richard: Great. So, from now on, please try to practice communication skills when handling your affairs with other departments.

In order to draw a lot of attention in the competitive market to increase its high profile, the PR office intends to entrust a media image design company with the task of making an online video. A group of people are discussing what they would like to see in the video.

John: Regarding the video making, three aspects need to be included: website setting, story making, and budget planning. What do we have so far?

Elaine: I've talked to the image design company about our requirements and they will help us design stories and make several videos. I've also talked to the accounting department about the budget for the video.

Louis: The company will help us set up a website and design the homepage for us too. There will be 5 different videos, two to five minutes long, rotating on the site.

John: Very good. When will they complete this project?

Louis: The manager of the media company said that they would give us a rough cut of the video and a draft of the homepage design in one month. After review, they will revise and launch them on the website. I estimate that the video of EZ Company will be set up on the web in two months.

John: Excellent! I'm looking forward to seeing them. By the way, when they are writing the story, they need to emphasize the harmonious atmosphere of the office.

Louis: You bet!

Powerful word bank

owner 所有人	coordination 協調	ineffective 無效率的
misunderstanding 誤解	lift 振作	morale 士氣
interim 臨時的	attendee 出席者	aware 知道的
affect 影響	overall 全部的	propose 提出
valuable 有價值的	decline 下降	dare 敢
remind 提醒	encounter 遭遇	regularly 定期地
conduct 實施	warehouse 倉庫	constructive 建設性的
insufficient 不足的	convey 傳達	competitive 競爭的
intend 打算	entrust 委託	media 傳播媒體
image 形象	aspect 方面	budget 預算
homepage 首頁	rotate 旋轉	draft 草稿
revise 修訂	estimate 估計	emphasize 強調

Useful phrases

as well as 不但...而且	in the meantime 同時
in person 親自	in stock 存貨
from now on 從現在開始	high profile 高知名度
rough cut 初步剪接	set up 使（器械、機器等）準備使用
You bet! 當然！	

Discussion

1. What do you do when you have communication problems with your colleagues?

2. What do you do when you don't quite understand the task designated to you in the workplace?

Supplementary information

Problems appearing in the factory

1. The time for ordering forging materials takes too long.
   採購鍛品花的時間太久了。

2. Semi-finished products in the lathe process are always out of stock and the production time can't be controlled.
   車床半品庫存一直無法補齊亦無法掌握生產時間。

3. Not being familiar with the merchandise and products.
    針對採購及生產之產品不瞭解。

4. No substitute for someone who takes a leave of absence.
    請假時沒代理人。

5. The factory requires materials but someone failed to order them.
    有存量需求但會遺漏採購。

6. Poor control on subcontractors that include lathe, grinding, word rolling, and heat treatment industries.
    沒辦法掌控協力廠商（協力廠商：車床、研磨、滾字、熱處理等加工廠）。

The Process of Manufacturing　原物料製程

metal materials → forging → lathing → grinding → word rolling → heat treatment → sandblasting → vibrating → plating → warehousing

鐵材 → 鍛造→車床 → 研磨 → 滾字 → 熱處理 → 噴砂 → 振動 → 電鍍 → 入庫

 **MEMO**

UNIT 16	eBay Online Shopping 線上購物

Useful expressions

1. Online shopping has become the trend of the times.

2. It's very convenient for people to shop online.

3. Internet fraud happens frequently. We need to be very careful when we go shop online.

4. On the eBay website, there are many different categories for shoppers to select from.

5. Online shopping means shopping in a virtual shop.

Words and phrases

online shopping 線上購物	trend 趨勢	convenient 方便的
fraud 欺騙	category 種類	virtual 虛擬的

Dialogue

Richard, the boss, asks Lily to order a specific hand tool from eBay because he wants to compare it with a certain product manufactured in his factory. Lily is not familiar with the operation of online purchasing abroad so she asks James for help.

Lily: Hi, James. Are you free now? If possible, could you please come to my office in a minute? I need your help to show me how to access to eBay's website. The boss asked me to purchase something on eBay.

James: No problem. I'm just trying to get a cup of coffee. Would you like one too?

Lily: No. Thanks.

In Lily's office...

James: So, let's access eBay's website first. By the way, before searching for the items, we need to register on eBay so that we can do business with them. Okay, what do you want to see now?

Lily: The boss needs to order a specific hand tool produced in the U.S. Can we go to the hand tool pages?

James: Sure. There are a variety of hand tools displayed on the screen. Which one does the boss require?

Lily: Let me see. Oh, I found it. That's the one the boss wants. Wait, there's another similar one. I think I'd better order both items so that we can have better understanding of this kind of product. Could you help me order them online? Here's the credit card the boss gave me.

James: Okay. How many pieces do you need?

Lily: I think one for each is enough.

James: So, I'll choose and click this item and pay for it now. In addition to the products, we also need to pay for shipping. They will be delivered in two weeks. So, now, I'll press the 'confirm & pay' button.

Lily: Yes, please do. Thank you very much. I've learned how to make an online purchase. I can do it by myself next time if the boss asks me to order overseas products online.

A few days later, Lily calls James about the eBay order.

Lily: Hi, this is Lily. Is James there?

James: Hello, this is James. What's up?

Lily: Remember we ordered some hand tools on eBay a few days ago. I've gotten an e-mail saying that the purchase failed. Could you help me find out what's going on?

James: No problem. I'll come to your office right away.

Lily and James are sitting in front of the computer.

James: Let's access to the eBay website again.

Lily: So, do you know what the problem is?

James: Hmm...it says that the products we are ordering are out of stock now and it suggests that we should replace them with similar ones.

Lily: I think I'd better ask the boss before taking the next step.

James: Sure. If you need any help, just call me.

Lily: Thank you. I will.

Powerful word bank

compare 比較	purchase 購買	abroad 到國外
access 進入	item 項目	register 註冊
screen 螢幕	choose 選擇	replace 取代

Useful phrases

search for 尋找	a variety of 各種各樣的
What's up? 怎麼回事	out of stock 無庫存

Discussion

1. Online business is an opportunity for people who intend to be their own boss. How can they conduct their business successfully?

2. If your employer asked you to buy an object that cannot find in Taiwan, what would you do?

3. There are many shopping websites on the Internet. How do you examine their reliability?

Supplementary information

Tips for shopping online

· If you are not in a hurry, you'd better shop around for the best deal.

· Using cash on delivery for the payment is more secure.

· Make a shopping list first or else you might waste your time and money on unnecessary items.

 **MEMO**

UNIT 17 Fellowship between Colleagues 同事情誼

Useful expressions

1. When I am busy, my colleagues will give me a hand.

2. Treat colleagues as family and everything will go smoothly.

3. Together, everyone achieves more. Be nice to colleagues, and they will be nice in return.

4. Sometimes, some of us will go to beautiful camping areas to spend the whole weekend together.

5. We will share with one another some useful information presented on the Internet.

Words and phrases

give sb. a hand 幫忙	treat 對待	smoothly 流暢地
in return 回報	camping area 露營區	

Dialogue

It's around ten in the morning. Lily is busy contacting the subcontractor about ordering packing boxes. The phone rings and she goes to answer it.

Lily: Hello, Lily speaking.

Penny: Hi, Lily. It's Penny. We are going to order lunch boxes. Do you need anything to eat?

Lily: Oh, time goes by so fast. It's almost lunch time. Thank you for reminding me. Can I have a box with fish?

Penny: All right. How about having lunch together? We are going to order some special food online during the lunch break.

Lily: Okay. Let me know when it's time for lunch. I need to get back to work.

At lunch time...

Kelly: I forgot it's Thursday today. It's my vegetarian day. Who would like my chopped pork?

James: Ha, I think I can help you but I'll need to go to the gym to run on the treadmill after work.

Lily: What are you going to buy online today?

Penny: The Moon Festival is coming soon and we'd like to order some moon cakes online.

Kelly: Yes, and I was told that one specific moon cake is a hot item online lately and we can get a good deal by group buying.

Penny: Are you interested in joining us, Lily?

Lily: It's a good idea. Hmm...I think I may need several boxes of moon cakes. I can give them to my family and friends.

James: Other than moon cakes, I also need pomelos for the festival.

Kelly: I was told that production is reduced this year because of the typhoon so they've become expensive. Are you sure you want to buy them?

James: Yes, my grandmother likes them very much. I'll buy some for her. Does anyone want to join me?

Penny: How many pomelos are there in one box? And when will I receive them?

James: There are six in each box and they'll be delivered once the merchandise order is confirmed.

Penny: Okay. I need two boxes.

Kelly: Me too.

Lily: Give me five, please. I have a big family to take care of.

James: So, now, we can access the website to order our items.

Lily: It's one o'clock now. I need to make some business phone calls. Thank you very much.

Penny: When I receive the goods, I'll let you know.

Lily: By the way, how do I pay? By credit card or cash?

Penny: We usually pay cash on delivery. Credit card fraud happens every day in various forms. You can't be too careful.

Lily: Yes, I agree. Let me know how much I need to pay.

Penny: OK!

Powerful word bank

contact 聯繫	subcontractor 外包商	treadmill 跑步機
hot 熱門的	form 形式	pomelo 柚子
reduce 減少	cash 現金	

Useful phrases

packing box 包裝盒	lunch break 午休時間	chopped pork 豬排
Moon Festival 中秋節	group buying 團購	other than 除了
pay cash on delivery 貨到付款		

Discussion

1. What are the advantages of maintaining fellowship between colleagues?

2. How do you cultivate relationships with colleagues?

3. How important is it to have a pleasant atmosphere in the office?

 **MEMO**

UNIT 18 Organizing the Product Exhibition 會展籌備

Useful expressions

1. There are many things that need to be taken care of to exhibit products at the trade show.

2. Who is going to organize this big event?

3. We can ask our clients about their exhibition experiences.

4. It will be a large-scale exhibition and we have to make sure to reserve the booth we'd like in advance.

5. There will be a variety of hand tools exhibited at the show.

6. In addition to the exhibits, we also need to prepare the posters, flyers, and small gifts.

7. Don't forget to make invitations to invite our clients to visit.

Words and phrases

exhibit 展示（品）	trade show 商展	organize 安排
large-scale 大規模的	booth 攤位	poster 海報
flyer 傳單	make invitations 邀請	

Dialogue

The annual Taiwan Hardware Show is coming up in October. People are talking about this event in the office.

Lily: The annual hardware show will be held next week. Who is going this year? James, are you interested in visiting?

James: Actually, I just visited a hardware show in Shanghai with Penny last month. And I'm organizing the pamphlets and flyers collected from the show. So I'm not going again this time.

Lily: What did you think about the show, Penny?

Penny: It was a large-scale show. There were hundreds of manufacturers. We could not visit all of them because there were really too many. I found many booths exhibiting hand tools which were similar to ours.

Lily: Well, I think I'll take a day off to go to the hardware show by myself. The boss hopes that we can exhibit our products one day in the near future. He also indicates that I have to arrange the booth by the time the show starts. So, if possible, please lend me a hand.

After visiting the show, Lily shares her experience with her colleagues in the office.

Lily: It's a real big show. I have to say it's like 'people mountain, people sea' as we say in Chinese. It's very impressive. I found there were many foreigners attending the show too.

Christin: So, what would you think if our products are exhibited there?

Lily: Well, I think firstly I need to improve my English competency so that I can deal with foreigners on the spot. They looked at things carefully and kept asking questions.

Christin: Other than English, what else do you need to do? It'll be a brand new project we need to work on now. So, Penny, what's your opinion?

Penny: I think we need to design impressive posters that will attract visitors' attention to our booth so they'll do business with us.

James: We may need to prepare some gifts for the attendees and interview them for some information about their companies and requirements. Of course, don't forget to exchange business cards.

Christin: It's a good idea to collect potential customers' background information. So, James, please design a questionnaire and put it on my desk by next Monday. Thank you. By the way, what about the location of our booth?

Penny: It should be placed near the entrance so that it can easily catch the visitors' eyes.

Christin: I think we need to have another meeting to discuss the exhibition plan.

Lily: Yeah, I think so. Having a successful exhibition is very important to the reputation of our products. I need to spend more time planning it. Luckily, under such a strong team, I believe we will have a successful exhibition when the day comes.

Powerful word bank

actually 實際上	pamphlet 小冊子	arrange 安排
impressive 予人深刻印象的	interview 訪問	questionnaire 問卷
location 位置	entrance 入口	reputation 名聲

Useful phrases

Taiwan Hardware Show 臺灣五金展	hundreds of 數以百計的
by oneself 獨自	on the spot 在現場
brand new 全新的	potential customer 潛在客戶
catch sb.'s eye 某事引起某人的注意	

Discussion

1. What kinds of trade shows are held annually in Taiwan? Who participates in these kinds of event?

2. What kinds of corporations in Taiwan participate in overseas trade shows to demonstrate their products?

3. Where does the annual Taiwan Hardware Show take place?

4. Where is the center of hardware production in Taiwan?

Supplementary information

參展相關作業

1. 參展前要先熟悉當次參展的產品，因為大多數的客戶會看目錄及詢問產品相關問題。工作事先分配好，並先準備好行銷的相關資料，包括：產品目錄、規格表、報價表、海報及掛牌。此外要留意大會的訊息，按照大會的規定去進行。

2. 接下來要跟裝潢公司討論裝潢，如何讓客人對公司的攤位有驚豔的感覺。

3. 展覽結束後最重要的是整理及收回參展的產品。有些公司會當場便宜賣出，所以要看產品要如何出口，再做後續的處理。

4. 有些參展大型機台的公司在會展結束後須撤回機台，所以需留技術人員拆卸機台，並指揮堆高機及請卡車運送等作業。

5. 空檔時間，參觀和公司相關產業的攤位，觀摩別家的機台，以及公司需要買的附件的參展廠商。

6. 參展時要特別注意安全，尤其是展示大型機台，有些顧客會跨到
    機台裡，產品的機密性也要注意，還要留意各個不同客人的報價
    及相關問題之詢問。所以，最好準備記事本，隨時記錄重要的
    人、事、時、地、物等的訊息，留作公司重要的參考資料。

7. 有機會時，在展場現場請顧客填寫問卷，並提供公司的聯繫資料
    予對方。

問卷範例

國家	
公司	
職位	
姓名	
Email	
memo	

1. 你對哪個商品有興趣？是否需提供樣品？	
2. 你是□代理商□貿易商□直客 □其他 _____ □代理品牌_____	
3. 可以分享你的販售通路嗎？及主要市場？	
4. 請問你以前買過此類商品嗎？	
5. 針對產品，你有特殊要求嗎？	
6. 請問你希望產品如何寄送？需要任何認證嗎？	□空運□海運□其他_____
7. 請問你的國家的進口關稅是多少？	

 **MEMO**

UNIT 19 Exhibiting the Product at the Fair　產品參展

Useful expressions

1. What products does your company produce?

2. Here's the sample.

3. Please allow me to demonstrate for you.

4. Do you have a special request for the product?

5. How would you like to have the product sent?

6. Do you need any certification?

7. What is the import tariff of your country?

8. Could you fill in this survey, please?

9. I need to set everything up before the exhibition starts!

10. There are audio players available to help with touring the exhibition.

Words and phrases

sample 樣本	demonstrate 示範操作	certification 證明
import 進口	tariff 關稅	survey 調查
audio player 聲音播放器	available 可利用的	

Dialogue

EZ Company intends to exhibit its products at the annual Taiwan Hardware Show. Lily is in the booth standing by. A foreign visitor comes to the booth. It's show time.

Lily: Hi, good morning. How may I help you?

Visitor: Hi. I'm interested in the tool boxes displayed on the table.

Lily: Oh, yes. They are our new products.

Visitor: Can you tell me their purpose?

Lily: Sure. Those boxes are stackable. So they will be neat when you stack up all boxes.

Visitor: Yes, they really do. But, I think it will be heavy if all the tool boxes are stacked up together and it will be hard to move around.

Lily: Well, rollers can be fixed to the bottom of the box at the customer's request. And they come with a brake device.

Visitor: Yeah, it will be easier to move that way. So, how different are the three boxes?

Lily: This is the drawer-type, that is the lower-height non-drawer-type, and the third one is in progress now. It is a non-drawer type but has the same height as the first one. The drawer-type box contains the tray, dividers, and an EVA pad. They aren't found in the non-drawer type box.

Visitor: Thanks. So, what else do they have?

Lily: See, the handle's pull strength has been tested and it can lift up objects weighing up to 120 kilos.

Visitor: How do you stack up and take apart the tool box?

Lily: There are locks in the notches set on both sides of the box. Unlock them and move it. It's easy to lift the box on both sides to stack it up or take it apart. And, the handling position has an ergonomic design.

Visitor: I've got one more question. Why doesn't the switch work smoothly?

Lily: It's for security. If it is too smooth, the lid may become loose and open unexpectedly. I almost forgot to mention that the materials conform to European Union (EU) regulations. They are environmental-friendly, reused and recycled materials.

Visitor: Thank you very much for your detailed introduction.

Lily: If you have further questions or are interested in our products, please contact me. Here's my card. By the way, could you please fill in this survey questionnaire?

Visitor: Sure...I'm done. Thanks. Bye-bye.

Lily: Thank you. Have a good day.

Powerful word bank

stackable 可堆疊的	neat 整齊的	roller 滾輪
fix 安裝	brake 煞車	device 裝置
drawer 抽屜	height 高度	contain 包含
tray 托盤	divider 隔板	pad 墊
handle 提把	weigh 稱起來	kilo 公斤
lock 上鎖	notch 凹口	ergonomic 人體工學的
switch 開關	security 安全	lid 蓋子
loose 鬆的	unexpectedly 意外地	environmental-friendly 保護生態環境的
reuse 重複使用	recycle 回收利用	detailed 詳細的
further 進一步的		

Useful phrases

stand by 準備行動	tool box 工具箱
stack up 把...疊放起來	in progress 進行中
pull strength 拉力	lift up 舉起
take apart 拆開	European Union(EU) 歐盟

PART **2**

Discussion

1. What do the exhibitors need to do when they are in the exhibition hall?

2. When the exhibition is ending, what do exhibitors do with their displayed objects? The objects may be housewares, auto parts, tools, or machines.

3. For what purposes do the exhibitors conduct the visitor survey at the exhibition?

Supplementary information

Useful terms 實用語詞

importer 進口商	local dealer 當地的賣家
dealer; distributor 經銷商	agent 代理商
trader 貿易商	manufacturer 廠商
agent brand 代理品牌	sale channel 販售通路
leading market 主要市場	air transport 空運
ocean shipping 海運	product layout 產品布置
product introduction 產品介紹	product quotation 產品報價
booth 攤位	exhibition hall 展覽場
best-selling 最暢銷的	

Three important factors for introducing your products 產品介紹的 3 個要點

1. Know your own products well. 充分瞭解自家產品。

2. Help customers select their merchandise. Let them know what programs/ promotion you provide for the products.
   協助顧客挑選商品及告知產品的促銷方案。

3. Give follow-up contact information for after-sales service.
   提供售後服務資訊。

PART **②**

UNIT 20　The End of the Year Party 尾牙宴

Useful expressions

1. Have you ever heard of the end of the year party before?

2. Do you have a similar party in your country?

3. In general, a big company will hold a large party for their employees at the end of the year.

4. They spend a lot of money on paying famous stars or singers to perform.

5. Sometimes, the boss will donate a brand new car for a lucky draw.

6. After the party, this year is almost over and a new year is just ahead of us.

Words and phrases

in general 通常	perform 表演	donate 捐獻
lucky draw 抽獎	ahead of 在...之前	

Dialogue

EZ Company is going to hold the end of the year party for their employees in appreciation of their hard work. Mr. Tu, the director of Human Resource, is in charge of organizing the party. He asks some colleagues for help.

Mr. Tu: James, Allen, and Penny, I need your help for the end of the year party. Can you give me some ideas? It is held once a year and I hope it will impress everybody.

James: No problem. How do we split the work?

Allen: Yeah, I like the party. It's fun. I can arrange the entertainment program. What budget do we have?

Mr. Tu: The boss didn't give me an exact number, but I think we just follow last year's. What do you think about going to the same restaurant? Their dishes are delicious and the prices are reasonable. Many colleagues were satisfied with it last year. If it is okay, I'll make a reservation as early as possible. It's the end of the year party season and many restaurants are fully booked already.

Penny: Do we have a lucky draw in the party? I like that part. It's very exciting and fun.

Mr. Tu: Yes, we can arrange that part too. But Penny, can you ask the cooperative manufacturers to sponsor the gifts?

Penny: Me again? All right, I'll do it and I will ask other colleagues to help me wrap all the gifts.

Mr. Tu: Thank you. James, can you help make the invitations and take care of the food and refreshments. I'll give you the guest list later.

James: Sure. I can ask the others to help me. And I will go to the restaurant with Penny on the weekend to see what they have and how the food tastes.

Mr. Tu: I appreciate it. Allen, what activities do you plan to provide at the party?

Allen: As usual, we will have singing, dancing, and a magic show. I know some of our colleagues have very good voices and are good at dancing. I'll ask volunteers to show off their talents that day. I may need to look for a magician.

Penny: Do you need me to find someone for you? My friend's friend is an amateur magician.

Allen: That's excellent. Yes, please do.

Mr. Tu: Hmm...it seems that the party doesn't have any problems. Thank you very much for your help.

At the end of the year party, James and Penny are host and hostess. They are both standing on the stage.

Penny: Good evening, ladies and gentlemen. My name is Penny.

James: My name is James. We are your host and hostess tonight.

Penny: First of all, we would like to represent all employees in thanking our boss for holding this party for us.

James: We also appreciate the cooperative manufacturers generously donating a lot of gifts for the lucky draw. Now, let's welcome our boss to give us a few words.

After the speech, it's show time.

Penny: Please enjoy the delicious food and enjoy the performance by our colleagues.

The lucky draw is an interlude between the entertainment acts. It's a very successful party, and everybody is very excited and has a wonderful evening.

PART **2**

Powerful word bank

split 分擔	entertainment 娛樂	program 節目
reasonable 合理的	wrap 包，裹	refreshments 茶點
voice 聲音	volunteer 志願者	talent 才藝
magician 魔術師	amateur 業餘從事者	host 節目主持人
hostess 女主持人	stage 舞臺	represent 代表
interlude 插入的事物		

Useful phrases

be satisfied with 對...感到滿意	as usual 像往常一樣
magic show 魔術表演	be good at 擅長於
show off 賣弄	first of all 首先

Discussion

1. What is the best way for an employer to reward their employees at the end of the year?

2. What does it mean to serve the chicken dish in the end of the year dinner party?

 **MEMO**

產品功能示範及職場相關業務操作流程

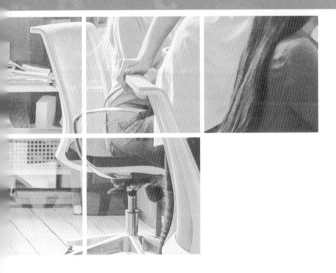

UNIT 01 Hand Tools Demonstration
手工具操作步驟示範

1. The T-bar　T 型棘輪扳手

(1) Press the button of the T-bar to connect the quick-release extension bar.

(2) Then, put the end of the T-bar on the spline socket. They will connect to each other automatically.

(3) Pull the adapter back to remove the spline socket. The adapter is at the end of the quick-release extension bar.

The features of the T-bar

(1) The difference between the new style and the traditional style is that the new style is easier to store and saves more space. 節省收納的空間。

(2) The smart LED lights are easier to store, carry and provide light.
小精靈(the smart LED light)方便收納、攜帶和照明。

(3) The quick-release extension bar can be quickly changed to fit various sizes of sockets. 快脫接桿可快速替換各尺寸的套筒。

(4) It provides 20 kinds of BIT. 提供 20 種樣式的 BIT。

(5) With the quick-release extension bar and socket, the T-bar can easily access deep and narrow points/spots.
T Bar 連接快脫接桿再加上套筒，可提供深孔作業。

2. The smart LED lights 小精靈 LED 燈

(1) Put the smart LED lights on the pedestal and the lights will turn on automatically.
小精靈放上底座，自動亮燈。

(2) Rotate the lights 90 degrees to right/left and the lights will turn off.
90°旋轉至左右兩側面，自動熄燈。

(3) Elevate the pedestal 90 to 140 degrees, and the lights will reach wide angles.
小精靈底座可以往上轉 90~140°方便調整所需照亮的角度。

(4) The smart LED lights can join the quick-release extension bar to light up the deep and narrow point.
小精靈可放置快脫接桿上提供陰暗處深孔照明。

(5) The smart LED lights can be put on the rim of a hat to give light.
可夾在帽緣提供陰暗處的光線照明。

(6) The pedestal can store two spare batteries.
底座可存放兩個備用電池。

3. Functions of the Go-through Ratchet　穿透棘輪扳手

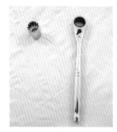  

(1) Put the spline socket in the go-through ratchet. Push the pick to the right or left and the socket is able to turn in different directions. Remove the socket by pushing it with the thumb.

(2) Put the bit in the adapter. Then put the set in the go-through ratchet. It becomes a screw driver.

(3) Put the quick-release adapter in the go-through ratchet. It becomes a regular ratchet handle.

(4) Press the pin to connect the socket adapter. Then it can adapt to various sizes of sockets.

(5) Put the bit in the one-quarter (1/4) adapter. Then connect the set with the nut driver. It becomes another screw driver.

(6) Connect the spline socket with the nut driver. Press the blue button at the end of the handle to light up the deep and narrow spot/point.

(7) The handle can be used as a flashlight.

(8) The spline socket can be used on six different shapes of screws. In addition, it can be used in a narrow and limited space.

(9) Connect the adapter with the three-eighths (3/8) go-through ratchet. Put the one-quarter (1/4) spline socket in it. The tool can be used on smaller sized screws.

4. Dr. (driver) low profile ratchet 薄型 C 扣式葫蘆柄

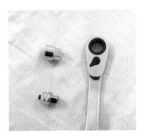  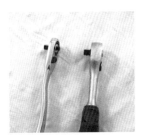

(1) This is a new-style ratchet. There is a C-shaped metal ring inside the head of the ratchet, so it is called a C-shaped ratchet.

(2) The low profile ratchet needs to go with the socket developed by EZ Company.

(3) There are several nicks around the rim of the socket developed by the company so that the C-shaped ratchet can buckle up the socket.

(4) There are two ways to use. The first one is to directly connect with the socket developed by EZ Company. However, unlike the traditional one with the push button, this one needs the thumb to release the socket. The second way is that the handle can connect a single adapter and then a socket: either traditional length, 25 mm or self-developed, 17 mm.

PART **3**

(5) The length of the socket is a self-setting specification. The socket of the EZ Company can connect to the handles produced by other companies.

(6) After connecting to a single adapter, the new-style handle can connect to a stubby bit socket.

(7) The head of the handle is thinner which can save more space and is easier to reach narrower spaces.

The traditional ratchet

(1) There is only one use for the traditional handle: connect   the socket directly. The head is thicker.

(2) The length of the traditional socket is longer. The EZ Company offers shorter sockets.

 **MEMO**

UNIT 02 Introduction to a Product Example　產品解說範例

Stacking tool boxes 堆疊盒

The features of the tool box

1. The box is stackable. 可以層層堆疊。

2. There is a honeycombed design on the inner side of the lid and at the bottom of the box. 盒蓋內面及箱底採蜂巢式設計。

3. An empty drawer-type tool box weighs 3 kilograms net.
    空盒（附抽屜）淨重 3 公斤。

4. The preferred color for the tool box can be customized but it needs to conform to the MOQ (Minimum order quantity).
    顏色可客製化，但是須符合 MOQ（Minimum order quantity 最低訂購量）。

5. The features of honeycombed design include a heavy-duty body and attractive appearance. 蜂巢式設計特點為耐摔、耐重、美觀、較堅固。

 **MEMO**

UNIT 03 從接單至出貨的流程：
以油封為例

1. 客戶詢價，我們報價。通常是新產品或是訂購數量有變動才會詢價，一般客戶會直接發訂單過來。

2. 談好價格後，客戶會發訂單過來。

3. 我們開 proforma invoice (PI) 給客戶簽章，PI 的功能算是訂單的確認書，上面會寫品項、材質、數量、單價、出貨日期及其他備註等等。

4. 收到客戶簽章後，開始進行採購及生產作業。我們拿到簽回的 PI 後，就會打「訂單製造通知單」，將外部資料變成內部資料，採購會根據製造通知單進行採購，然後產生「流程單」讓接下來的部門知道如何跑流程。因為油封有各種型式，處理方法有很多，流程單上面會寫批號、客戶代號、出貨日期、如何包裝、用什麼料號生產、料多重、多長、多厚、鐵殼的材質、彈簧的材質、是否需要其他加工、如：研磨、噴漆等等，有些客戶有特殊要求也會寫在上面。

5. 原物料進廠後要「進料檢驗」，沒問題後排上生產。

6. 生產前要先「試模」，看看這樣的料生產出來的狀況行不行。

7. 品保驗過看過試模的東西，沒問題就可進行生產。生產時品保會自己找時間做巡檢，可能兩小時、三小時一次，防止產生太多的不良品，例如：尺寸沒有進公差、或是其他問題。

8. 生產好的東西，要整修就先整修，要打毛邊就打。

9. 品檢。

10. 包裝。在進行包裝的時候有產品最終檢驗，給品保驗尺寸。

11. 出貨。打訂單製造通知單。

　　聯絡客戶出貨相關事宜。貨物有問題通常客人就會來詢問。

　　國內出貨比較簡單，提供客戶要的資料及叫貨運來就可以。

　　國外出口需跟客戶端確認如何出貨，準備文件（報關用或是客人要的文件）。

(1) 海運

要去簽船。通常都請合作的報關協助，告知他們我們安排哪家客戶的出貨、何時結關日、箱數、棧板數、重量、材積，然後報關行會去跟貨物代理人（貨代，forwarder, fwd）進行 booking，通常國外客戶都會有指定 fwd。

(2) 空運 1

fwd 的空運。客戶如果有跟 fwd 合作，50Kg 以上的貨就有可能用這個方式出貨，運費會比較便宜。

(3) 空運 2

快遞(DHL, UPS, FEDEX, TNT)。客戶如果有其中之一的帳號，就用該帳號出貨。當客戶沒有快遞帳號又想走快遞的時候，我們會先報價給客人，等同意運費後就進行出貨。

a. DHL：很貴，但速度真的很快，品質有保障，例如寄到美國印第安納州韋恩堡隔天就到了。

b. UPS：也是很貴，跟 DHL 有得比。但如果量比較多，談合約的時候 UPS 會給折扣的優惠，運送時間一樣快。

c. Fedex：價格中等，運送時間中等，服務還算不錯。

d. TNT：在還沒有 UPS 的合約時運費最便宜，但遞送時間最慢，客服態度比較不理想，但是因為它很便宜，大多數的客人都要 TNT，可是如果出問題就很麻煩。

　　無法海運的話，我們都比較喜歡客人出快遞，因為叫快遞只需要付運費(door to door service)，快遞來收貨，運送到客戶公司門口。如果用空運，我們還要把貨送到機場，因此還需要付錢給貨運行，又是一個成本。客戶本身也需要負擔從機場到公司的運費，而且我們還要去跟貨代 booking，確認送到哪個倉儲，就有些麻煩，有些貨代的窗口拖拖拉拉，要三催四請的。快遞現在都有電子提單，只需要在網路上填資料，就有人來收貨了，非常方便實用。

　　出貨完畢後就給客戶發票、出貨資料、追蹤號等等，只要輸入追蹤號，就可以得知貨目前的情況及到了哪裡。

 MEMO

附錄 ❶ 相關字彙及片語

A

adaptor 接頭

air-powered extension bar
氣動接桿

annealing 退火

assemble 組合

air-powered adaptor 氣動接頭

air impact socket 氣動套筒

arrival date 到貨日

assembly 裝配

B

ball 鋼珠

beneficiary 受益人

bit hold BIT 條

blow case 吹氣盒

ball screw 滾珠螺桿

bit adapter 彈套

block 滑塊

burr 毛邊

C

caliper 游標卡尺

chain steel 煉鋼

chrome-plated 鍍鉻

color 上色

conveyor 輸送帶

cutting oil 切削油

carton 紙箱

chamfer 倒角

clearance date 結關日

conventional manual lathe
傳統車床

cutting 切斷

CNC (Computerized Numerical Control) 電腦數值控制工具機

CAM (Computer Aided Manufacture) 電腦輔助製造

CSR (Corporate Social Responsibility) 企業社會責任

D

debossing 浮字

deep socket 長套筒

delivery date 交貨日

diamond rasp 鑽石銼刀

dispatching 調度

deburr 除毛邊

defective product 不良品

delivery order 出貨單

direct machining parts
直接加工零件

double-groove type 雙溝

3/8" drive go-through ratchet 穿透式棘輪板手

E

earplug 耳塞

embossing 沉字

end cap 端蓋

end seal 刮油片

extension socket 穿透接桿

electroplated 電鍍的

embossing methods 壓字方式

end mills 端銑刀

extension bar 接桿

F

foam 泡棉

forging 鍛造

fonts cost 字模費用

forklift; forklift truck 堆高機

G

glossy 鏡面

go-thru socket 穿透套筒

grease 潤滑油脂

grinding repair 磨修

go-thru bit adapter 穿透彈套

go-thru spline socket
穿透齒型套筒

grind 研磨

gross weight 毛重

H

Hex point extension bar 外六角接桿

I

imperial system 英制
inventory statement 庫存表

inventory 庫存量

J

joint 油管接頭

K

knurled 滾花

L

lab 檢驗室
lapping 精磨
lead time 交貨時間
light bar 光棒

labor cost 工資
lathe 車床
L-handle L 桿
linear guideway 線性滑軌

M

machine arms 機器手臂
matte 霧面
mercury fog 水銀霧
micrometer 分厘卡

manganese phosphate 磷酸錳
measured yaw 量測偏擺
metric measure/system 公制
nut driver 套筒起子

N

net weight 淨重

noise test 音頻測試

O

oil row 油排
outer box 外箱

overhead travelling crane 天車
outsourcing process 委外加工

P

plating 電鍍
press-fit 壓配
process zone 加工區
purchase order 採購單

polish 亮面；拋光
processing 加工流程
pull testing 拉力測試
purchase requisition 請購單

Q

quantity 數量

quick-release extension bar
快脫接桿

quick-release adapter 單快脫接頭

R

rail 線軌

robotic arm 機械手臂

rotating speed 轉速

rustproof oil 防鏽油

reset 程式復歸

roller 滾筒

rust 鏽斑

S

sandblasting 噴砂

scrap 報廢（品）

screw tap 螺絲攻

shipment 裝船，出貨

sliding T-bar 滑桿

spanner handle 貫通大方桿

spline socket 齒型套筒

stock 庫存

straightness 真直度

swift code 銀行代碼

satin finished 霧面

scraper 金屬刮板

shallow socket 短套筒

show room 成品間

socket adapter 扣環套筒接頭

spark-plug socket 火星

stacker crane 堆高機

straightening 校直

surface treatment 表面處理

T

terms of trade 貿易條件

torque test 扭力測試

touch LED Disc light 小精靈

trial order 試單

tooling cost 模具費用

torque wrench 扭力扳手

touch LED Disc light set pedestal
小精靈座

U

unit box 單箱

universal joint adaptor 萬向

V

vendor 供應商

ventilation system 通風設備

vibration 震動

W

warehousing 入庫

wiper 刮刷器

wobble two-way extension bar
搖接桿

wrench 扳手

MEMO

附錄 II 單字音節發音法

Unit 01 Cli-ent Re-cep-tion 客戶接待

Words and phrases

ap-**point**-ment（尤指正式的）約會	ride 搭乘	zone 地區
be **in**-te-res-ted in 對...感興趣	co-o-pe-**ra**-te 合作	**e**-le-va-tor 電梯
next to 在...旁邊	water **foun**-tain 飲水機	**hall**-way 走廊

Powerful word bank

in-**form** 告知	**cli**-ent 客戶	**col**-league 同事
re-**ceive** 接待	ac-**cu**-mu-late 累積	re-**cep**-tion 接待
cour-te-ous-ly 有禮貌地	means 方法	**stra**-te-gy 策略
hos-pi-**ta**-li-ty 款待	**in**-ter-com 對講機	**sig**-nal 發信號
un-**lock** 開啟	au-to-**ma**-ti-cal-ly 自動地	ad-**mi**-nis-tra-tor 行政官員
her-bal 草本的	re-pre-**sen**-ta-tive 代表	**com**-pli-ment 恭維
treat 款待	re-**serve** 保留	

Useful phrases

in time 及時	at the same time 同時	re-<u>cep</u>-tion room 會客室
<u>ge</u>-ne-ral <u>ma</u>-na-ger 總經理	<u>busi</u>-ness card 名片	make a re-ser-<u>va</u>-tion 預約
pick up 用汽車接某人	by then 到那時	

Unit 02 Pre-sen-<u>ta</u>-tion Skills 簡報技巧

Words and phrases

pre-sen-<u>ta</u>-tion 介紹	in-<u>clude</u> 包括	<u>pro</u>-duct 產品
pro-<u>duce</u> 生產		

Powerful word bank

e-<u>vent</u> 事件	<u>pre</u>-vi-ous 先前的	<u>pro</u>-per-ly 恰當地
su-per-<u>vi</u>-sor 監督人	<u>con</u>-tent 內容	<u>thor</u>-ough 周密的
pre-<u>sent</u> 提出	<u>flu</u>-id-ly 流暢地	greet 問候
<u>au</u>-di-ence 觀眾	<u>brief</u>-ly 簡潔地	or-ga-ni-<u>za</u>-tion 組織
<u>em</u>-pha-size 強調	<u>fea</u>-ture 特色	im-<u>press</u> 使感動

Useful phrases

make a pre-sen-**ta**-tion 做簡報	pass by 經過	in ad-**di**-tion 此外
eye **con**-tact 眼神接觸	dress up 穿上盛裝	**fac**-to-ry tour 工廠參觀
first shot 首次嘗試		

Unit 03 Fac-tory Ins-pec-tion 驗廠

Words and phrases

do-cu-ment 文件	re-**quest** 要求	in-**spect** 檢查
watch your step 留心您的腳步	gauge 測量儀器	e-va-lu-**a**-tion 評估
cer-ti-fy 證實	**de**-sig-nate 委任	

Powerful word bank

of-**fi**-cial 正式的	**au**-tho-rize 授權給	e-**xa**-mine 檢查
Ger-ma-ny 德國	di-**splay** 陳列	**ob**-ject 物體
main-ly 主要地	lo-**cate** 把...設置在	**ex**-port 輸出
lo-go 標識	ap-**pa**-rent-ly 顯然地	ex-**pand** 擴充
am-**bi**-tious 有雄心的	ven-ti-**la**-tion 通風	**re**-le-vant 有關的
im-**me**-di-a-te-ly 直接地	**in**-put 投入	**sta**-tion-ery 文具
lap-top 筆記型電腦	dis-**turb** 打擾	ring 打電話

Useful phrases

show room 展覽室	take a look at 看一看
OEM (O-ri-gi-nal E-quip-ment Ma-nu-fac-tu-rer) 委託代工	con-fe-rence room 會議室

Unit 04 · In-dus-tri-al Health and Safe-ty 工業衛生與安全

Words and phrases

fire truck 救火車	scene of the fire 火場	flame 火焰
shoot out 像子彈一般衝出	me-tal sheet 鐵皮	in case 以防萬一
self-help 自助	cause 引起	loss pro-per-ty 財產損失
pro-hi-bit 禁止	in-doors 在室內	un-less 除非
de-sig-na-ted a-rea 指定的範圍	ground 地面	slip-pe-ry 滑的
war-ning sign 警告標誌	place 放置	be e-quipped with 配備有…
sprink-ler sys-tem 自動噴水滅火系統	smoke de-tec-tor 煙霧探測器	

Powerful word bank

in-**dus**-tri-al 工業的	**ac**-ci-dent 事故	**da**-mage 損害
pre-**vent** 防止	di-**sas**-ter 災害	con-**vene** 召集
fre-quent 時常發生的	**ca**-te-go-ry 種類	**re**-gu-lar-ly 定期地
fire-**proof** 防火的	**coa**-ting 塗層	up-**date** 更新
va-lid 有效的	**check**-list 核對清單	ne-ver-the-**less** 然而
pre-**ven**-tive 預防的	**mea**-sures 措施	oc-**cur**-rence 發生
clean-li-ness 潔淨	au-**tho**-ri-ty 管理機構	**to**-lu-ene 甲苯
sa-ni-**ta**-tion 公共衛生	**oi**-ly 油的	**walk**-way 走道
lo-**ca**-tion 位置	**ob**-vi-ous 明顯的	**han**-ging 掛著的
de-**vice** 裝置	ig-**nore** 忽視	**noi**-sy 嘈雜的
flam-ma-ble 易燃的	**li**-quid 液體	**draw**-back 缺點
in-de-**pen**-dent-ly 獨立地	**ma**-nu-al 手冊	**han**-dy 便利的
o-pe-ra-tor 操作者	de-**fec**-tive 有缺陷的	dis-qua-li-fied 使不合格
con-**tai**-ner 容器	**ha**-zar-dous 有危險的	**sub**-stance 物質
nod 點頭	e-**sta**-blish 建立	**ar**-chi-tect 建築師
a-**ban**-don 丟棄	rent 租用	en-**sure** 保證

Useful phrases

set up 建立	work on 從事
en-<u>vi</u>-ron-men-tal <u>mo</u>-ni-tor-ing 環境監測	<u>pro</u>-duct <u>la</u>-bel-ing 產品標誌
such as 例如	e-<u>mer</u>-gen-cy <u>e</u>-xit light 緊急出口燈
es-<u>cape</u> guide light 逃生引導燈	fire de-<u>tec</u>-tor 火警探測器
fire a-<u>larm</u> 火警警報器	e-va-cu-<u>a</u>-tion plan 逃生配置圖
fire ex-<u>tin</u>-gui-sher 滅火器	<u>car</u>-ry out 執行
in the <u>in</u>-te-rest of 為了…	<u>loa</u>-ding and un-<u>loa</u>-ding <u>a</u>-rea 裝／卸貨區
keep clear 保持通暢	at all times 隨時
<u>au</u>-to-ma-ted ex-<u>ter</u>-nal de-<u>fi</u>-bril-la-tor 自動體外心臟去顫器	o-pe-<u>ra</u>-tion <u>pro</u>-cess 操作步驟
<u>se</u>-nior <u>wor</u>-ker 資深員工	next to 在…旁邊
make sure 確定	note down 記下
semi-finished <u>pro</u>-duct 半成品	in par-<u>ti</u>-cu-lar 尤其是
in ad-<u>di</u>-tion 此外	on track 正軌；進入狀況
<u>fo</u>-cus on 集中於	

Unit 05　Waste Treat-ment　廢棄物處理

Words and phrases

waste 廢（棄）物	li-censed 有執照的	treat-ment 處理
re-move 搬開	hand tool 手工具	scrap 碎片
i-ron fi-lings 鐵屑	re-cy-cling 回收	raw ma-te-ri-al 原料
re-use 再使用	ef-fec-tive-ly 有效地	a-mount 數量
pro-tect 保護	re-gu-late 管理	a set of 一組；一套
dis-po-sal 處理	me-thod 方法	treat 處理
in ac-cor-dance with 根據		

Powerful word bank

glance 一瞥	mo-ni-tor 顯示器	screen 螢幕
ac-ci-den-tal-ly 意外地	tri-cy-cle 三輪腳踏車	re-cy-cla-ble 可回收物
an-noy 惹惱	se-cu-ri-ty 安全	vul-ne-ra-bi-li-ty 弱點
tres-pass 擅自進入	col-lect 收集	e-xist 存在
thought-less 欠考慮的	ma-nu-fac-tu-rer 製造業者	il-le-gal-ly 非法地
dump 傾倒	con-ta-mi-na-tion 汙染	aw-ful 極糟的
soil 土壤	harm 傷害	fa-ci-li-ty 場所

un-<u>wan</u>-ted 不需要的	rust 鐵鏽	<u>use</u>-less 無用的
<u>plas</u>-tic 塑膠	<u>par</u>-ti-cle 微粒	o-<u>ri</u>-gi-nal 原始的
<u>ho</u>-nes-tly 誠實地	de-<u>ci</u>-sion 決定	<u>ob</u>-so-lete 淘汰的
store 貯存	<u>ware</u>-house 倉庫	<u>tem</u>-po-ra-ri-ly 臨時地

Useful phrases

door <u>ac</u>-cess con-<u>trol</u> 門禁管制	from door to door 挨家挨戶地
a-<u>bide</u> by 遵守	in name <u>on</u>-ly 表面上的；掛名的
What's up? 怎麼啦？	no <u>lon</u>-ger 不再
clear up 清理	turn into 使變成
hang up 掛斷電話	for a while 一會兒
free up 騰出	

Unit 06 End-less Wor-king Hours　無止盡的工作

Words and phrases

<u>end</u>-less 無休止的	<u>work</u>-load 工作量	<u>oc</u>-to-pus 章魚
at a time 一次	stressed 感到有壓力的	tense 繃緊的
<u>sche</u>-dule 日程安排表	<u>pac</u>-ka-ging 包裝（業）	get be-<u>hind</u> 落後
o-ver-<u>time</u> 加班		

Powerful word bank

place 開出（訂單）	de-li-ver 運送	ship 運送
goods 貨物	hire 僱用	wage 薪水
en-ti-tle 給...權力（或資格）	the-o-re-ti-cal-ly 理論上	late-ly 最近
po-li-cy 政策	em-ploy-er 雇主	pur-pose 目的
re-duce 減少	go-vern-ment 政府	in-come 收入
re-la-tive-ly 相對地	ef-fec-tive 有效的	re-so-lu-tion 解決
har-mo-ni-ous 和諧的	re-la-tion 關係	com-plete 完成
post-pone 使延期		

Useful phrases

hold on 不掛電話	get to-ge-ther 聚集	hang up 掛斷電話
ca-su-al la-bo-rer 臨時工	hu-man re-source 人力資源	e-xempt em-ploy-ee 責任制員工
ac-cor-ding to 根據	La-bor Stan-dards Act 勞動基準法	ma-nu-fac-tu-ring cost 製造成本
as a re-sult 結果	la-bor u-nions 工會	af-ter all 畢竟
catch up to 趕上		

Unit 07   Te-le-phone Man-ners   電話禮節

Words and phrases

leave a <u>mes</u>-sage 留言   take a <u>mes</u>-sage 留言   call sb. back 回電

spell 拼寫

Powerful word bank

ap-<u>pro</u>-pri-a-te-ly 適當地   ease 使安心   di-<u>rect</u> 指點

<u>per</u>-so-nal 個人的   al-<u>low</u> 允許   <u>pa</u>-tient 有耐心的

di-<u>rect</u>-ly 直接地   in-<u>ti</u>-mi-da-ting 令人膽怯的   in-<u>ten</u>-tion 意圖

tone 語氣   task 任務   con-<u>nec</u>-tion 連接

ex-<u>ten</u>-sion 電話分機

Useful phrases

make a mis-<u>take</u> 犯錯   <u>of</u>-fice hours 上班時間

role play 角色扮演   put sb. through 把電話接過來

right away 立刻

Unit 08 Mi-grant Wor-kers　移工管理

Words and phrases

mi-grant wor-ker 移工	Viet-nam 越南	most-ly 大多數地
hu-man re-sources a-gen-cy 人力銀行	re-cruit 徵募	li-ving quar-ter 宿舍

Powerful word bank

ap-pear 出現	re-cent-ly 最近	shor-tage 缺少
is-sue 問題	man-pow-er 人力	mid-dle-aged 中年的
neigh-bor-hood 鄰近地區	ex-change 交換	de-lay 耽擱
cause 使發生	re-quire-ment 必要條件	warn 警告
ac-com-mo-da-tion 住處	sup-port 支持	a-djust 調整
ve-ge-ta-ri-an 吃素的	con-firm 確認	Thailand 泰國
In-do-ne-sia 印尼	in-ter-pre-ter 口譯員	com-pul-so-ry 必須做的
re-gu-la-tion 規定	per-for-mance 成果	main-te-nance 維持
phy-si-cal 身體的	fre-quent-ly 頻繁地	launch 發出

Useful phrases

<u>spe</u>-cial as-<u>sis</u>-tant 特別助理	a <u>num</u>-ber of 一些
<u>suf</u>-fer from 受...困擾	be <u>wil</u>-ling to 願意
vi-ce <u>ver</u>-sa 反之亦然	for <u>ins</u>-tance 例如
be fa-<u>mi</u>-li-ar with 熟悉	back up 支持
in the long run 從長遠來看	take <u>ac</u>-tion 採取行動
hot pot 火鍋	main course 主菜
<u>quan</u>-ti-ty of 大量	room and board 食宿
staff <u>quar</u>-ter 員工宿舍	lunch box 便當
<u>qua</u>-li-ty con-<u>trol</u> 品質控制	pay at-<u>ten</u>-tion to 關心
kill time 打發時間	used to 過去經常

Unit 09　Help <u>Wan</u>-ted　徵才

Words and phrases

con-<u>ven</u>-tion-al 傳統式的	<u>in</u>-dus-try 行業	pre-<u>fer</u> 寧願（選擇）
<u>ra</u>-ther than 而不是...	<u>now</u>-a-days 現今	re-su-<u>me</u> 履歷表
es-<u>sen</u>-tial 必要的	<u>at</u>-ti-tude 態度	<u>punc</u>-tu-al 準時的
<u>for</u>-mal-ly 正式地	<u>in</u>-tern 實習生	

Powerful word bank

cer-tain 某一	ac-coun-ting 會計	there-fore 因此
di-rec-tor 主管	co-wor-ker 同事	quit 停止
hi-tech 高科技	e-xhaust 使精疲力盡	a-ward 授予
o-pe-rate 運作	spe-ci-fic 特定的	pro-gram 程式
ma-jor 主修	e-xag-ge-rate 誇大	com-pe-ten-cy 能力
si-mi-lar 類似的	in-di-cate 指出	grade 成績
po-si-tion 職務	sa-la-ry 薪水	browse 瀏覽
col-lect 收集	qua-li-fied 合格的	ob-tain 獲得

Useful phrases

ea-ger for 渴望	In-dus-tri-al En-gi-nee-ring and Ma-nage-ment 工業工程與管理
re-late to 與...有關	clas-si-fied ads 分類廣告
make up 給...排版	take sth. into con-si-de-ra-tion 考慮到
con-form to 符合	ap-pli-ca-tion form 申請表

Unit 10 In-service Trai-ning Pro-gram
員工在職訓練

Words and phrases

of-fer 提供	take a trip 旅行	af-ter work 下班
take care of 處理	prac-ti-cal 實用的	ap-ply for 申請
grant 准予		

Powerful word bank

se-mi-nar 討論會	ex-pe-ri-enced 有經驗的	talk 演講
ac-tual 實際的	per-form 執行	sa-tis-fac-to-ri-ly 令人滿意地
follow-up 採取進一步行動	affair 業務	quit 辭職
an-nounce 發布	as-sign 指定	par-ti-ci-pate 參加
pro-po-sal 提案	ap-prove 批准	via 經由
ad-vanced 高級的	mo-di-fy 修改	le-vel 程度
in-ter-me-di-ate 中級的	quiz 測驗	con-ve-ni-ent 方便的
ti-ring 令人疲倦的		

APPENDIX

Useful phrases

<u>gra</u>-du-ate from 從…畢業	<u>mi</u>-li-ta-ry <u>ser</u>-vice 兵役
work <u>pro</u>-gress 工作進展	fit in 使適應
get fa-<u>mi</u>-liar with 熟悉	re-<u>sult</u> in 導致
<u>half</u>-<u>way</u> through …到一半時	take up the post 出任
right away 立刻	fire drill 消防演習
the <u>pub</u>-lic 公眾	<u>bul</u>-le-tin board 布告欄
sign up 報名登記	no pain, no gain 一分耕耘，一分收穫

Unit 11
Pro-duct De-sign and Ma-nu-fac-tu-ring
產品設計與製造

Words and phrases

<u>cus</u>-to-mize 訂做	ac-<u>cor</u>-ding to 根據	<u>buy</u>-er 買主
ins-<u>pire</u> 激勵	<u>hard</u>-ware 五金器具；硬體	<u>soft</u>-ware 軟體
spe-<u>ci</u>-fic 具體的	ad-<u>mi</u>-ni-stra-tive sup-<u>port</u> 行政上的支援	

Powerful word bank

<u>sam</u>-ple 樣本	pe-<u>ci</u>-fi-cal-ly 特別地	ef-<u>fect</u> 效果
ex-pla-<u>na</u>-tion 說明	res-<u>pon</u>-si-ble 認真負責的	<u>cu</u>-ri-ous 渴望知道的

<u>con</u>-crete 具體的	pro-<u>pose</u> 提出	proof 樣張
<u>com</u>-pe-tent 有能力的	<u>ex</u>-tra 額外的	<u>por</u>-tion 部分
sup-<u>pli</u>-er 供應商	<u>ur</u>-gent-ly 緊急地	<u>life</u>-guard 救生員
beg 懇求		

Useful phrases

meet sb's need 符合某人的需要	find out 發現
be a-<u>ware</u> of 意識到	torque-<u>tes</u>-ting 扭轉力測試
a batch of 一組；一群；一批	fall be-<u>hind</u> 落後
in hot <u>wa</u>-ter 有麻煩	No way! 當然不！
pass on 傳遞	

Unit 12　Em-ploy-<u>ee</u> <u>Wel</u>-fare　員工福利

Words and phrases

stable 平穩的	sys-te-<u>ma</u>-tic 有系統的	<u>be</u>-ne-fit 好處
in-<u>cen</u>-tive <u>pay</u>-ment 獎勵津貼	<u>an</u>-nu-al 一年一次的	in-<u>cen</u>-tive <u>tra</u>-vel 獎勵旅遊
ex-<u>pense</u> 費用	pa-<u>ren</u>-tal leave 育嬰假	

Powerful word bank

pale 蒼白的	<u>cli</u>-nic 診所	re-<u>co</u>-ver 恢復
<u>ou</u>-ting 短途旅遊	in-di-<u>vi</u>-du-al 個人的	<u>sce</u>-ne-ry 風景
<u>sca</u>-ry 可怕的	cruise（坐船）旅行	book 預訂
charge 索價		

Useful phrases

<u>sto</u>-mach <u>up</u>-set 腸胃不適	had <u>bet</u>-ter 最好
leave of <u>ab</u>-sence 請假	sick leave 病假
<u>Hu</u>-man Re-<u>source</u> <u>of</u>-fice 人資室	<u>me</u>-di-cal cer-<u>ti</u>-fi-cate 醫療證書
<u>an</u>-nu-al leave 年休假	white-<u>wa</u>-ter <u>raf</u>-ting 泛舟
look <u>for</u>-ward to 期待	as well 也
by air 乘飛機	high <u>sea</u>-son 旺季
in ad-<u>vance</u> 預先	It's a shame. 真是可惜
ma-<u>ter</u>-ni-ty leave 產假	leave wi-<u>thout</u> pay 留職停薪

Unit 13 <u>An</u>-nu-al In-<u>cen</u>-tive <u>Tra</u>-vel　員工旅遊

Words and phrases

re-<u>lief</u> 慰藉	stress 壓力	<u>dis</u>-tance 距離
<u>at</u>-mos-phere 氣氛	<u>spring</u>-time 春天	

Powerful word bank

main 主要的	<u>for</u>-tu-nate-ly 幸運地	reach 達到
goal 目標	<u>ge</u>-ne-rous 慷慨的	<u>spon</u>-sor 贊助
ex-<u>pe</u>-ri-enced 有經驗的	off-shore 離岸的	<u>is</u>-land 島嶼
<u>fer</u>-ry 渡輪	<u>sea</u>-gull 海鷗	e-<u>co</u>-lo-gy 生態
u-<u>nique</u> 獨特的	bait 誘餌	<u>fire</u>-work 煙火
<u>gor</u>-geous 華麗的	please 討好	ap-<u>pre</u>-ci-ate 感激
re-<u>charge</u> 再充電		

Useful phrases

in charge of 負責	<u>tra</u>-vel <u>a</u>-gen-cy 旅行社	tour bus 遊覽車
go <u>snor</u>-kel-ing 浮潛	in-ter-<u>ti</u>-dal zone 潮間帶	have a <u>bar</u>-be-cue 烤肉
go <u>fi</u>-shing 釣魚	<u>fi</u>-shing rod 釣竿	<u>fi</u>-shing boat 漁船
<u>Luc</u>-ky you! 你真幸運！		

Unit 14 Ne-go-ti-a-ting a Bet-ter Price through E-mail 議價商業書信

Words and phrases

swift 迅速的	re-ply 答覆	ac-cept 接受
heart-felt 衷心的	a-po-lo-gy 道歉	re-gards 關心
stay in touch 與...保持聯繫		

Powerful word bank

ne-go-ti-ate 協商	vo-lume （生產，交易等的）量	quote 報價
pro-mise 承諾	fol-low-up 後續的	deal 交易
cir-cum-stance 情況	af-ford 支付得起	in-su-rance 保險
ex-pire 到期	in-ven-tory 存貨	sa-tis-fac-tion 滿意
in-spire 激勵	cons-tant-ly 不斷地	steel 鋼
quar-ter 季	im-ple-ment 實施	strict 嚴格的
per-son-nel 員工	pro-ces-sing 加工	plas-tic 塑膠
com-pe-ti-tion 競爭	re-tail 零售	at-tack 攻擊
dis-count 折扣	pro-mo-tion 促銷	en-cour-age 鼓勵
strength 實力	com-pe-ti-tor 競爭者	per-ma-nent-ly 永久地

fluc-tu-<u>a</u>-tion 波動	<u>slight</u>-ly 稍微地	<u>com</u>-pro-mise 妥協
cal-cu-<u>la</u>-tion 計算結果	<u>fi</u>-nal 最後的	claim 聲稱
sin-<u>cere</u>-ly 誠懇地		

Useful phrases

due to 由於	raw ma-<u>te</u>-ri-al 原料	make <u>pro</u>-gress 進展
lead to 導致...後果	<u>mar</u>-ket share 市場占有率	ever be-<u>fore</u> 以前
bear the price 承擔價格	ex-<u>change</u> rate 外匯率	in fact 事實上
<u>u</u>-nit cost 單位成本	o-<u>ri</u>-gi-nal price 原價	

Unit 15 — Ef-<u>fec</u>-tive <u>In</u>-ter-de-part-<u>men</u>-tal Com-mu-ni-<u>ca</u>-tion 部門之間的有效溝通

APPENDIX

Words and phrases

<u>work</u>-place <u>e</u>-thic 職場倫理	a-<u>chieve</u> 實現
<u>hin</u>-der 阻礙	im-ple-men-<u>ta</u>-tion 實踐
in-ter-<u>per</u>-so-nal re-<u>la</u>-tion-ship 人際關係	<u>con</u>-flict 衝突
<u>na</u>-tu-ral 自然的	

Powerful word bank

ow-ner 所有人	co-or-di-**na**-tion 協調	in-ef-**fec**-tive 無效率的
mis-un-der-**stan**-ding 誤解	lift 振作	mo-**rale** 士氣
in-te-rim 臨時的	at-**ten**-dee 出席者	a-**ware** 知道的
af-**fect** 影響	**o**-ver-all 全部的	pro-**pose** 提出
va-lu-able 有價值的	de-**cline** 下降	dare 敢
re-**mind** 提醒	en-**coun**-ter 遭遇	**re**-gu-lar-ly 定期地
con-**duct** 實施	**ware**-hou-se 倉庫	con-**struc**-tive 建設性的
in-suf-**fi**-cient 不足的	con-**vey** 傳達	com-**pe**-ti-tive 競爭的
in-**tend** 打算	en-**trust** 委託	**me**-di-a 傳播媒體
i-mage 形象	**as**-pect 方面	**bu**-dget 預算
home-page 首頁	**ro**-tate 旋轉	draft 草稿
re-**vise** 修訂	**es**-ti-mate 估計	**em**-pha-size 強調

Useful phrases

as well as 不但...而且	in the **mean**-time 同時
in **per**-son 親自	in stock 存貨
from now on 從現在開始	high **pro**-file 高知名度
rough cut 初步剪接	set up 使（器械、機器等）準備使用
You bet! 當然！	

Unit 16 E-bay <u>On</u>-line <u>Shop</u>-ping 線上購物

Words and phrases

<u>on</u>-line <u>shop</u>-ping 線上購物	trend 趨勢	con-<u>ve</u>-ni-ent 方便的
fraud 欺騙	<u>ca</u>-te-go-ry 種類	<u>vir</u>-tu-al 虛擬的

Powerful word bank

com-<u>pare</u> 比較	<u>pur</u>-chase 購買	a-<u>broad</u> 到國外
<u>ac</u>-cess 進入	<u>i</u>-tem 項目	<u>re</u>-gis-ter 註冊
screen 螢幕	<u>si</u>-mi-lar 類似的	re-<u>place</u> 取代

Useful phrases

search for 尋找	a va-<u>ri</u>-e-ty of 各種各樣的
What's up? 怎麼回事	out of stock 無庫存

Unit 17 <u>Fel</u>-low-ship be-<u>tween</u> <u>Col</u>-leagues 同事情誼

Words and phrases

give sb. a hand 幫忙	treat 對待	<u>smooth</u>-ly 流暢地
in re-<u>turn</u> 回報	<u>cam</u>-ping <u>a</u>-rea 露營區	

Powerful word bank

con-<u>tact</u> 聯繫	sub-con-<u>trac</u>-tor 外包商	<u>tread</u>-mill 跑步機
hot 熱門的	form 形式	<u>po</u>-me-lo 柚子
re-<u>duce</u> 減少	cash 現金	

Useful phrases

<u>pac</u>-king box 包裝盒	lunch break 午休時間	chopped pork 豬排
Moon <u>Fes</u>-ti-val 中秋節	group <u>buy</u>-ing 團購	<u>o</u>-ther than 除了
pay cash on de-<u>li</u>-ve-ry 貨到付款		

Unit 18 <u>Or</u>-ga-ni-zing the <u>Pro</u>-duct E-xhi-<u>bi</u>-tion 會展籌備

Words and phrases

ex-<u>hi</u>-bit 展示（品）	trade show 商展	<u>or</u>-ga-nize 安排
large-scale 大規模的	booth 攤位	<u>pos</u>-ter 海報
<u>fly</u>-er 傳單	make in-vi-<u>ta</u>-tions 邀請	

Powerful word bank

<u>ac</u>-tu-al-ly 實際上	<u>pamph</u>-let 小冊子	ar-<u>range</u> 安排
im-<u>pres</u>-sive 予人深刻印象的	<u>in</u>-ter-view 訪問	ques-tion-<u>aire</u> 問卷
lo-<u>ca</u>-tion 位置	<u>en</u>-trance 入口	re-pu-<u>ta</u>-tion 名聲

Useful phrases

Tai-<u>wan</u> <u>Hard</u>-ware Show 臺灣五金展	<u>hun</u>-dreds of 數以百計的	by one-<u>self</u> 獨自
on the spot 在現場	brand new 全新的	po-<u>ten</u>-tial <u>cus</u>-to-mer 潛在客戶
catch sb.'s eye 某事引起某人的注意		

Unit 19 E-<u>xhi</u>-bi-ting the <u>Pro</u>-duct at the Fair 產品參展

Words and phrases

<u>sam</u>-ple 樣本	<u>de</u>-mon-strate 示範操作	cer-ti-fi-<u>ca</u>-tion 證明
im-<u>port</u> 進口	<u>ta</u>-riff 關稅	sur-<u>vey</u> 調查
<u>au</u>-di-o <u>play</u>-er 聲音播放器	a-<u>vai</u>-la-ble 可利用的	

Powerful word bank

<u>stac</u>-ka-ble 可堆疊的	neat 整齊的	<u>rol</u>-ler 滾輪
fix 安裝	brake 煞車	de-<u>vice</u> 裝置
<u>draw</u>-er 抽屜	height 高度	con-<u>tain</u> 包含
tray 托盤	di-<u>vi</u>-der 隔板	pad 墊
<u>han</u>-dle 提把	weigh 稱起來	<u>ki</u>-lo 公斤
lock 上鎖	notch 凹口	er-go-<u>no</u>-mic 人體工學的
switch 開關	se-<u>cu</u>-ri-ty 安全	lid 蓋子
loose 鬆的	un-ex-<u>pec</u>-ted-ly 意外地	en-vi-ron-<u>men</u>-tal-<u>friend</u>-ly 保護生態環境的
re-<u>use</u> 重複使用	re-<u>cy</u>-cle 回收利用	de-<u>tailed</u> 詳細的
<u>fur</u>-ther 進一步的		

Useful phrases

stand by 準備行動	tool box 工具箱
stack up 把...疊放起來	in <u>pro</u>-gress 進行中
pull strength 拉力	lift up 舉起
take a-<u>part</u> 拆開	Eu-ro-<u>pe</u>-an <u>U</u>-ni-on (EU) 歐盟

Unit 20 The End of the Year Par-ty 尾牙宴

Words and phrases

in ge-ne-ral 通常	per-form 表演	do-nate 捐獻
luc-ky draw 抽獎	a-head of 在...之前	

Powerful word bank

split 分擔	en-ter-tain-ment 娛樂	pro-gram 節目
rea-son-able 合理的	wrap 包，裹	re-fresh-ments 茶點
voice 聲音	vo-lun-teer 志願者	ta-lent 才藝
ma-gi-cian 魔術師	a-ma-teur 業餘從事者	host 節目主持人
hos-tess 女主持人	stage 舞臺	re-pre-sent 代表
in-ter-lude 插入的事物		

Useful phrases

be sa-tis-fied with 對...感到滿意	as u-su-al 像往常一樣
ma-gic show 魔術表演	be good at 擅長於
show off 賣弄	first of all 首先

MEMO

附錄 III Exercises 課後練習

Unit 01 Client Reception 客戶接待

A Answer the questions about the dialogue.

1. Why does Lily ask her colleague to help her receive the visitor?

2. What is the good strategy to receive quests?

3. Why does Matt arrive at the company earlier than the expected time?

4. What is Matt's plan in Taiwan?

5. Why does Matt think that he and Lily have known each for a while?

B Listen and circle the words that you hear.

administrator	zone	elevator	accumulate	client
representative	intercom	inform	cooperate	treat

C Pair work: dictate the words and phrases alternately to each other.

1._____ 2._____ 3._____ 4._____ 5._____

6._____ 7._____ 8._____ 9._____ 10._____

D **Pair work: work with a partner to correct the sentences.**

1. Lily serves Matt a cup of black coffee.

2. Matt is from Canada and he has been to Taiwan for several times.

3. Richard asks his driver to give Matt a ride to the hotel.

4. Lily was sick so she was not in her office to receive the visitor.

5. Matt is going to give Lily and Richard a treat at a restaurant.

Unit 02 Presentation Skills 簡報技巧

A Answer the questions about the dialogue.

1. Who will make a presentation for the foreign client?

2. What advice does Lily give to Kelly about the presentation?

3. What does a presenter need to do to start his/her presentation?

4. When greeting the audience, what does the presenter need to do?

5. What will Kelly do after the presentation?

B Listen and circle the words that you hear.

include	earplug	produce	presentation	warehouse
pointer	question	properly	greet	product

C Pair work: dictate the words and phrases alternately to each other.

1._____ 2._____ 3._____ 4._____ 5._____

6._____ 7._____ 8._____ 9._____ 10._____

D **Pair work: work with a partner to correct the sentences.**

1. The time for making a presentation should be limited to 30 minutes.

2. The presenter should face to the screen when making the presentation.

3. The presenter can use a pen to the targeted point.

4. Kelly is going to give Richard a treat after the presentation.

5. Kelly needs to dress up for the presentation.

Unit 03 Factory Inspection 驗廠

A Answer the questions about the dialogue.

1. Why do two inspectors go to EZ company?

2. What does Chris ask Lily for?

3. Where are the hand tools displayed?

4. Why does Chris think that the owner of the company works very hard?

5. What problems does Chris find in the production area?

B Listen and circle the words that you hear.

ring	require	official	certify	examine
authorize	inspect	request	expand	gauge

C Pair work: dictate the words and phrases alternately to each other.

1._____ 2._____ 3._____ 4._____ 5._____

6._____ 7._____ 8._____ 9._____ 10._____

D **Pair work: work with a partner to correct the sentences.**

1. The two inspectors are from France.

2. There are three factories in EZ company now.

3. The products produced by EZ company are mainly exported to the U.S.

4. The number of factory workers is declining.

5. While the inspection is in progress, the company will learn the result of the evaluation.

Industrial Health and Safety
工業衛生與安全

A Answer the questions about the dialogue.

1. Why does Christine call a meeting?

2. What are they going to work on for safety?

3. What required signs and systems of fire safety does David check regularly?

4. In the interest of sanitation, what does the factory have?

5. What is "AED" in English and in Chinese?

B Listen and circle the words that you hear.

noisy	prevent	flame	establish	update
slippery	coating	container	disaster	liquid

C Pair work: dictate the words and phrases alternately to each other.

1._____ 2._____ 3._____ 4._____ 5._____

6._____ 7._____ 8._____ 9._____ 10._____

D Pair work: work with a partner to correct the sentences.

1. People can smoke in the factory.

2. The company got a prize for giving the required physical examination to their workers who engaged in the noisy and flammable liquids areas.

3. The oily and slippery ground is acceptable in the factory.

4. The company had the building's public safety inspection when it was founded.

5. The staff quarters set up in the factory were remodeled.

Unit 05 Waste Treatment 廢棄物處理

A Answer the questions about the dialogue.

1. Why was the boss annoyed when he talked to Lily?

2. Where was the old woman from and what was she doing?

3. What do they do with useless plastic items?

4. Why does Kate call Lily?

5. Why does Lily call David?

B Listen and circle the words that you hear.

disposal	rust	scrap	security	store
annoy	obsolete	awful	original	facility

C Pair work: dictate the words and phrases alternately to each other.

1._____ 2._____ 3._____ 4._____ 5._____

6._____ 7._____ 8._____ 9._____ 10._____

D **Pair work: work with a partner to correct the sentences.**

1. For safety's sake, the door of the company should be kept open.

2. Polluted water and soil are fine for our health.

3. Kate is asking Lily to introduce her boyfriend to her.

4. The useless plastic items will be taken away by a waste clearance and treatment facility.

5. Lily is going to ship a batch of goods tomorrow.

Unit 06 Endless Working Hours 無止盡的工作

A Answer the questions about the dialogue.

1. Why do many workers complain to the government about the new policy?

2. Why do Lily and Vick need to work overtime?

3. What does Vick suggest Lily to help complete their work?

4. According to the Labor Standards Act, what should employer do for the overtime work?

5. Why do many employers not ask their employees to work overtime?

6. Who needs to find an effective solution to resolve the problems appeared in the workplace?

B Listen and circle the words that you hear.

wage	employer	workload	relation	tense
endless	ship	purpose	employee	deliver

C Pair work: dictate the words and phrases alternately to each other.

1.＿＿＿＿＿ 2.＿＿＿＿＿ 3.＿＿＿＿＿ 4.＿＿＿＿＿ 5.＿＿＿＿＿

6.＿＿＿＿＿ 7.＿＿＿＿＿ 8.＿＿＿＿＿ 9.＿＿＿＿＿ 10.＿＿＿＿＿

D **Pair work: work with a partner to correct the sentences.**

1. When employees work overtime, they usually get paid double time for overtime.

2. The company hires some casual laborers to work overtime to help pack the goods.

3. Exempt employees can get paid overtime if they work on the weekend.

4. Because of the new policy, the workers have more opportunities to work overtime.

5. Lily and Jenny are going to have dinner together after work.

Unit 07 Telephone Manners 電話禮節

A Answer the questions about the dialogue.

1. What advice does Lily give to Kate?

2. What does Kate need to do when the phone is ringing?

3. If you can't understand the foreign client's intention on the phone, what can you say?

4. What do you need to be when talking on the phone?

5. Why can't Louise hear Kate on the phone?

B Listen and circle the words that you hear.

intimidating	personal	extension	spell	ease
connection	tone	message	patient	direct

C Pair work: dictate the words and phrases alternately to each other.

1.＿＿＿＿＿ 2.＿＿＿＿＿ 3.＿＿＿＿＿ 4.＿＿＿＿＿ 5.＿＿＿＿＿

6.＿＿＿＿＿ 7.＿＿＿＿＿ 8.＿＿＿＿＿ 9.＿＿＿＿＿ 10.＿＿＿＿＿

D **Pair work: work with a partner to correct the sentences.**

1. Lily feels nervous and worries about her first day at work.

2. Kate feels excited when she learns that foreign clients may call the company sometimes.

3. When answering the phone, you ask the caller who he/she is firstly.

4. Louise hangs up the phone because he is not happy with Kate.

5. James is in his office when someone is calling him.

Unit 08 Migrant Workers 移工管理

A Answer the questions about the dialogue.

1. What are the two problems appeared in the company recently?

2. What does David suggest Christin to resolve the shortage of manpower?

3. Where are the migrant workers from in Jenny's company?

4. Where do the migrant workers live when they work for the company?

5. What compulsory requirements do migrant workers need to follow?

B Listen and circle the words that you hear.

frequently	recently	recruit	shortage	vegetarian
performance	appear	launch	delay	adjust

C Pair work: dictate the words and phrases alternately to each other.

1._____ 2._____ 3._____ 4._____ 5._____

6._____ 7._____ 8._____ 9._____ 10._____

D Pair work: work with a partner to correct the sentences.

1. Migrant workers are people who are from Taiwan.

2. Middle-aged women need to take care of their children and cannot get employment.

3. The company were warned in the last inspection about the work environment for migrant workers.

4. Jenny had a vegetarian hot pot and lemon juice for dinner.

5. After work, the company will order lunch boxes for migrant workers.

Unit 09 Help Wanted 徵才

A Answer the questions about the dialogue.

1. What departments are eager for new employees?

2. What does Louise's friend feel about working in the hi-tech industry?

3. Before hiring the job seekers, what is a good way to test them?

4. How does a company look for their potential employees?

5. What does Mr. Tu ask Jennifer to do about new employee recruitment?

B Listen and circle the words that you hear.

operate	collect	industry	punctual	salary
essential	intern	major	exaggerate	accounting

C Pair work: dictate the words and phrases alternately to each other.

1._____ 2._____ 3._____ 4._____ 5._____

6._____ 7._____ 8._____ 9._____ 10._____

D **Pair work: work with a partner to correct the sentences.**

1. Louise's friend was fired and is looking for a new job.

2. Louise's friend majored in Electrical Engineering.

3. Job seekers had better exaggerate their work competency in their resumes, so that they can find a good job.

4. It is acceptable to bring breakfast to go for a job interview.

5. Being a qualified intern, you had better not ask for help if you don't know how to deal with a thing.

In-service Training Program 員工在職訓練

A Answer the questions about the dialogue.

1. What is the Human Resource office going to do for the newcomers?

2. What time will the training programs be offered for the newcomers?

3. What will happen if the new employees are not familiar with their new job?

4. What are the three programs granted by the government?

5. How much do employees pay for the program they take?

B Listen and circle the words that you hear.

quiz	modify	tiring	perform	seminar
grant	actual	proposal	approv	quit

C Pair work: dictate the words and phrases alternately to each other.

1._____ 2._____ 3._____ 4._____ 5._____

6._____ 7._____ 8._____ 9._____ 10._____

D Pair work: work with a partner to correct the sentences.

1. A fire drill will be offered to the newcomers.

2. Mr. Tu will announce the information about the training programs to the employees at the meeting.

3. Three programs will last for one month.

4. James is going to take a 3D printing program.

5. Lily is going to take a basic English class.

Product Design and Manufacturing
產品設計與製造

A Answer the questions about the dialogue.

1. Why was James one hour late to the office?

2. Which department does James work for?

3. If James encountered problems in the process of making a new product, what would he do?

4. How does James create an item from zero to a concrete object?

5. Why did James miss a phone call from his friend yesterday?

B Listen and circle the words that you hear.

specific	urgently	customize	competent	hardware
supplier	propose	portion	lifeguard	effect

C Pair work: dictate the words and phrases alternately to each other.

1._____ 2._____ 3._____ 4._____ 5._____

6._____ 7._____ 8._____ 9._____ 10._____

D **Pair work: work with a partner to correct the sentences.**

1. James was late for work because he went to see a doctor.

2. Sometimes, James cannot make the items requested by his clients and gives up.

3. James's department is recruiting new employees because two guys are transferring to other departments.

4. James is too busy to help his colleagues from other departments.

5. James had dinner with his colleague yesterday.

Unit 12 Employee Welfare 員工福利

A Answer the questions about the dialogue.

1. What happens to James?

2. Why does Fanny suggest Christin to go to Hualian in the annual outing?

3. What can visitors do in Penghu?

4. Why can't Jennifer join the trip?

5. How much do employees need to pay for the trip?

B Listen and circle the words that you hear.

scenery	recover	systematic	expense	individual
incentive	benefit	cruise	outing	stable

C Pair work: dictate the words and phrases alternately to each other.

1._____ 2._____ 3._____ 4._____ 5._____

6._____ 7._____ 8._____ 9._____ 10._____

D **Pair work: work with a partner to correct the sentences.**

1. James has been suffering from a headache for months.

2. Lily enjoys going whitewater rafting a lot.

3. It is a low season so they don't need to book the tickets as early as possible.

4. James is taking leave with pay to take care of his father.

5. After maternity leave, Jennifer will come back to work.

Unit 13 Annual Incentive Travel 員工旅遊

A Answer the questions about the dialogue.

1. Why does the employer hold the annual incentive travel for his employees?

2. Who is in charge of the tour?

3. What do they do during the day?

4. Where do they go for the ecology tour?

5. How do they go fishing?

B Listen and circle the words that you hear.

relief	distance	bait	island	fortunately
atmosphere	recharge	unique	reach	appreciate

C Pair work: dictate the words and phrases alternately to each other.

1._____ 2._____ 3._____ 4._____ 5._____

6._____ 7._____ 8._____ 9._____ 10._____

D **Pair work: work with a partner to correct the sentences.**

1. EZ company holds a two-day tour for its employees.

2. The Human Resource office organizes all activities for the tour.

3. They have visited all offshore islands in Penghu.

4. Lily had caught three fish with her fishing rod.

5. The local government spent a lot of money on a three-minute fireworks show.

Negotiating a Better Price through E-mail
議價商業書信

A Answer the questions about the dialogue.

1. Why does Lily have to send a price increase notice to her client?

2. When Lily doesn't receive a follow-up e-mail from her client, what does she do?

3. In the e-mail, what are the reasons for increasing prices?

4. After receiving the note on price increase, what does the client do?

5. In order to maintain the business relationship with the client, what does Lily do?

B Listen and circle the words that you hear.

afford	retail	competitor	heartfelt	apology
accept	satisfaction	quote	negotiate	encourage

C Pair work: dictate the words and phrases alternately to each other.

1._____ 2._____ 3._____ 4._____ 5._____

6._____ 7._____ 8._____ 9._____ 10._____

D Pair work: work with a partner to correct the sentences.

1. Lily is the director of the Human Resource office.

2. In the e-mail, Lily said that the insurance was going to expire on February 20th.

3. Lily informed her client in the e-mail that the new price will be applied on orders effective March 31st, 2018.

4. Jack indicated in his e-mail that the good price is their strength in the market and low price is what keeps them growing.

5. Lily said in her e-mail that the final unit cost she could offer is 8.71.

Unit 15 **Effective Interdepartmental Communication 部門之間的有效溝通**

A Answer the questions about the dialogue.

1. Why does Richard hold an interim meeting at the lunch hour?

2. According to Lily, why is the implementation of work policies declining?

3. Why doesn't Henry's department dare take too many orders?

4. What does Richard think will make work easier?

5. Why does PR office intend to entrust a media image design company to make an online video?

B Listen and circle the words that you hear.

conduct	emphasize	lift	coordination	achieve
hinder	revise	budget	valuable	affect

C Pair work: dictate the words and phrases alternately to each other.

1._____ 2._____ 3._____ 4._____ 5._____

6._____ 7._____ 8._____ 9._____ 10._____

D Pair work: work with a partner to correct the sentences.

1. All employees will attend the interim meeting at noon in the conference room.

2. In a team, if one part goes wrong, it will not affect the overall situation.

3. Lily has to postpone the shipping date because the packaging gets behind.

4. There will be three different videos, five minutes long, rotating on the site.

5. When the image design company is writing the story, they need to emphasize the benefits of the office.

Unit 16 e-Bay Online Shopping 線上購物

A Answer the questions about the dialogue.

1. Why does Richard ask Lily to order an object from e-Bay?

2. Why does Lily ask James for help?

3. Before doing business with e-Bay, what does the shopper need to do?

4. When the shoppers want to buy the items selected on e-Bay, what button do they press?

5. Why does the purchase on e-Bay fail?

B Listen and circle the words that you hear.

convenient	virtual	fraud	abroad	compare
choose	register	replace	access	screen

C Pair work: dictate the words and phrases alternately to each other.

1._____ 2._____ 3._____ 4._____ 5._____

6._____ 7._____ 8._____ 9._____ 10._____

D **Pair work: work with a partner to correct the sentences.**

1. Lily has ordered three kinds of hand tools on the e-Bay.

2. Lily paid the objects selected with her credit cards.

3. Lily received the objects she ordered two weeks later.

4. e-Bay suggests that Lily should buy more pieces to get discount.

5. Using cash on delivery for the payment is more convenient.

Unit 17 Fellowship between Colleagues 同事情誼

A Answer the questions about the dialogue.

1. Why is Lily contacting the subcontractor?

2. Why does Penny call Lily?

3. Why does Kelly want to give her chopped pork to other colleagues?

4. What are they discussing about during the lunch break?

5. How will they pay the goods they ordered online?

B Listen and circle the words that you hear.

treat	smoothly	treadmill	contact	pomelo
reduce	cash	subcontractor	hot	form

C Pair work: dictate the words and phrases alternately to each other.

1._____ 2._____ 3._____ 4._____ 5._____

6._____ 7._____ 8._____ 9._____ 10._____

D **Pair work: work with a partner to correct the sentences.**

1. On Monday morning, Penny called Lily.

2. Lily would like to have chopped pork for lunch.

3. They are going to have dinner together after work.

4. There's no typhoon this year, so pomelos are cheap.

5. They are going to pay their goods by credit card.

Organizing the Product Exhibition
會展籌備

Unit 18

APPENDIX

A Answer the questions about the dialogue.

1. Where is Lily going to visit?

2. What is James working on after visiting the hardware show?

3. What does the boss hope to do in the near future?

4. What is Penny's opinion about exhibiting their products at the trade show?

5. Why do they want to interview the visitors at the show?

B Listen and circle the words that you hear.

exhibit	organize	flyer	invitation	reputation
arrange	actually	pamphlet	entrance	location

C Pair work: dictate the words and phrases alternately to each other.

1._____ 2._____ 3._____ 4._____ 5._____

6._____ 7._____ 8._____ 9._____ 10._____

D **Pair work: work with a partner to correct the sentences.**

1. The annual Taiwan Hardware Show is held in December.

2. James visited a hardware show in Bejing with Lily two months ago.

3. Penny is going to arrange the booth for the company at the show.

4. James thinks that they can exchange gifts at the show.

5. The best location of the booth is placed in the back of the exhibition hall.

Unit 19

Exhibiting the Product at the Fair
產品參展

A Answer the questions about the dialogue.

1. Who is standing by in the booth?

2. How can people easily move around the heavy stacking tool boxes?

3. What design does the handling positon have?

4. What kinds of materials are the tool boxes made of?

5. Before leaving, what was the foreign visitor asked to do?

B Listen and circle the words that you hear.

demonstrate	tariff	certification	contain	security
device	drawer	switch	recycle	brake

C Pair work: dictate the words and phrases alternately to each other.

1._____ 2._____ 3._____ 4._____ 5._____

6._____ 7._____ 8._____ 9._____ 10._____

D **Pair work: work with a partner to correct the sentences.**

1. The foreign visitor is interested in the hand tools displayed on the table.

2. When all tool boxes are stacked up together, they are easy to move around.

3. When the customers buy the stacking tool box, the rollers will be fixed on the bottom of the box.

4. The non-drawer-type box has the tray, dividers, and an EVA pad.

5. The materials of the box conform to SGS regulations.

Unit 20 The End of the Year Party 尾牙宴

A Answer the questions about the dialogue.

1. Why does Mr. Tu ask his colleagues to give him ideas about holding the party?

2. Why would Mr. Tu like to go to the same restaurant?

3. What will Penny do for the party?

4. What activities does Allen plan to have at the party?

5. Who donates the gifts for the lucky draw?

B Listen and circle the words that you hear.

perform	donate	entertainment	refreshments	host
reasonable	voice	interlude	program	split

C Pair work: dictate the words and phrases alternately to each other.

1._____ 2._____ 3._____ 4._____ 5._____

6._____ 7._____ 8._____ 9._____ 10._____

D **Pair work: work with a partner to correct the sentences.**

1. The purpose of holding the end of the year party is in appreciation of the employers.

2. The party is usually held twice a year.

3. The employer will sponsor the gifts.

4. Allen invited some famous singers to sing at the party.

5. The lucky draw was arranged at the end of the party.

 **MEMO**

 **MEMO**

 **MEMO**

國家圖書館出版品預行編目資料

職場英文 / 陳愛華著. – 二版. -- 新北市 : 新文京
開發, 2018.07
　　面 ；　公分

ISBN　978-986-430-412-7（平裝）

1. 英語　2. 職場　3. 讀本

805.18　　　　　　　　　　　　　　107009210

職場英文（第二版）　　　　（書號：E433e2）

編 著 者	陳愛華
出 版 者	新文京開發出版股份有限公司
地　　址	新北市中和區中山路二段 362 號 9 樓
電　　話	(02) 2244-8188（代表號）
Ｆ Ａ Ｘ	(02) 2244-8189
郵　　撥	1958730-2
初　　版	西元 2018 年 02 月 01 日
二　　版	西元 2018 年 07 月 15 日

New Wun Ching Developmental Publishing Co., Ltd.

New Age · New Choice · The Best Selected Educational Publications — NEW WCDP